Dancing Shoes

Another
Mt. Hope Southern Adventure

Book Three

Lynne Gentry

TRAVEL LIGHT PRESS

Dancing Shoes (Mt. Hope Southern Adventures, Book Three)

Copyright © 2017 by Lynne Gentry

All rights reserved.

Cover photo © 2017 Lynne Gentry

Cover Design by Castle Creations

Edited by Gina Calvert

ISBN: 978-0-9986412-2-5

ISBN: 0998641227

Sign up for Lynne Gentry's newsletter
and get **BONUS** material for FREE.
Details can be found at the end of **DANCING SHOES**.

Summary

When you realize you've been home all along...

The time has come for the widowed Leona Harper
to make a fresh start.
Leaving the parsonage means she'll need a home of her own.
Complicated finances force Leona to work with Saul Levy,
an uptight lawyer who questions
her makeover plans.
When a handsome old friend blows into town,
Leona is faced with her toughest decision yet.
Save the world, or dare to dance with a very unlikely partner?

Return to Mt. Hope and laugh until you cry.
Humor. Heart-melting romance. Hope.

MT. HOPE SOUTHERN ADVENTURES

Walking Shoes

Shoes to Fill

Dancing Shoes

Baby Shoes

Check out Lynne Gentry's

Sci-Fi/Time Travel Adventures

The Carthage Chronicles

Healer of Carthage

Return to Exile

Valley of Decision

A Perfect Fit

Shades of Surrender

For Anyone

who has ever prayed for a second chance.

Dancing Shoes

CHAPTER ONE

Leona dragged a strip of packing tape over the last moving box.

"Momma, you don't have to do this you know?" David took the tape dispenser from her hand. "There's plenty of room for you here."

Leona gazed into the conflicted eyes of her son. When had her little boy become such an admirable man? "David, you and your beautiful wife have bent over backwards to make me feel welcome, but there's not a parsonage in the world big enough for two pastor's wives."

Her relationship with her daughter-in-law was a tender shoot. Leona prayed untangling her roots and repotting her life would give Amy's love for her space to grow. However, maintaining good family relations wasn't the sole motivation pushing Leona out the door.

This move would test her on every level. Everyone had counseled her not to do anything rash for over a year. Except for taking on a paying job, she'd heeded their well-meaning advice. As she became more competent at the local newspaper, the grief-induced brain fog slowly began to lift. She still had those occasional gray days, but she was anxious to try out her wings and start to live again.

These last few months, she'd come to the conclusion that no matter how long she waited to begin her new life as a single woman, her decision to leave the parsonage would not only test her mettle, it would set tongues to wagging.

Other than wearing red heels whenever she pleased, she still steered clear of anything remotely capable of garnering disapproval from anyone, especially church members. Buying her own house, living her own life, dancing to her own tune would seem the natural progression of things for most widows putting their lives back together. For an ex-pastor's wife, however, striking out on her own could appear that she didn't appreciate the care the church had given her. That wasn't the case at all. She was very grateful. For her, launching herself into the world was throwing caution to the wind. Letting go of what she knew in order to embrace whatever God had waiting for her.

If J.D.'s death had taught her anything, it was that life was too short not to be lived to one's full potential. She'd thought it over and prayed until she was blue in the face. Moving was the next step on her journey.

David took her finished box and stacked it on the growing pile. "You're not in the way, Momma."

"It's time for you and Amy to make this house your home."

"Leona!" Roxie, the redheaded fireball from next door and Leona's best friend, yelled through the screen door. "You've got an offer on the suits."

Roxie swore that Leona's move across town wouldn't change their friendship, but they both knew they'd miss the gate between their shared fence.

"Be right there." Leona took her son's hand. "David, you've given me an extra eighteen months in the parsonage. That's six months beyond our original agreement. The only way I'm going to know if I've got my feet under me is to let go and leap." She didn't mention how David and Amy's increased trips to the city kept them so busy they probably wouldn't even miss her. Instead, she kissed his cheek. "It's time for me to make my own home." Before the tears she'd been holding back betrayed her, Leona sprinted out onto the large wrap-around porch.

Roxie was making change from an old metal tackle box

Leona had decided to keep. "Didn't know if you were flexible on the price," Roxie pointed to the young man thumbing through the suits hanging on the rope strung between two porch pillars.

"Wonder what Angus wants with a bunch of old suits," Leona whispered.

Roxie snapped the tackle box shut. "Let's ask him."

Leona followed Roxie as she blazed a trail between the people pawing through the odd assortment of knickknacks and furniture pieces Leona had chosen to part with. As they passed each prospective buyer, Leona handed out *good mornings* like she was an official church greeter.

Roxie scowled over her shoulder. "Hell's bells, Leona. You're hosting a garage sale, not a church social."

Old habits were hard to break, harder still when acceptance meant the definitive end of everything she knew.

These were the facts:

Those days were over.

Her pastor husband was dead.

She was no longer a pastor's wife.

It was no longer her job to make everyone feel welcome at the parsonage. She was handing off that responsibility to her new daughter-in-law. And she had full confidence Amy would do fine. This bright young nurse wasn't like her. Amy wouldn't allow herself to be saddled with the expectations of others. She was her own woman, a trait Leona wished she'd acquired earlier in life.

Roxie was right. How could she start a new life if she didn't let go of her old life? She should be trying to make sales and finish up the details for the move to the little house she'd bought. The 1960's ranch had only two small closets and ten fewer rooms than the huge parsonage she'd lived in for nearly twenty years. She'd chosen the claustrophobic layout for one purpose: less space...less room to feel alone.

Downsizing seemed like the next logical step. She didn't need a lot of space. Especially now that she was working at the newspaper full-time. Modyne made it her business to see that Leona's job assignments left her little energy for cleaning or entertaining.

So far, Roxie was the only person, other than her two children, who knew the real reason she'd put in an offer on a fixer-upper as far away from the church as possible. She could have built a dream home on the lake, but she preferred to keep the exorbitant amount of money J.D. had left her a secret. Years of pinching pennies was a habit as difficult to break as acting like a pastor's wife.

The kids wanted her to take her dream vacation to the Mediterranean, buy a new car, and purchase the parsonage.

Although she'd always wanted to travel, the van had close to three hundred thousand miles on it and might be good for fifty thousand more. She'd love to own the house she'd called home for nearly twenty years. But spending J.D.'s money on herself felt wrong, especially when there were so many needy causes in the world.

So she'd written a few checks. Secretly.

Her first anonymous contribution went to a missionary she and J.D. had known since college. A few months before J.D. died, Roy McGee lost his sweet wife to dengue fever. J.D. had asked the church board to finance Roy's much-needed sabbatical. Budget shortfalls cut the legs out from under J.D.'s argument. Oh, how J.D. would have enjoyed the surprise on Howard's face if he'd been the one who opened the anonymous offering envelope earmarked for Roy's return.

Next, she'd shared with her children. She'd paid off Maddie's medical school debt, bought her daughter a fully-furnished downtown condo for her medical residency stint, and spent a lavish sum on David and Amy's wedding, complete with the exotic honeymoon like the one J.D. had always promised they would take together one day.

She'd assumed church gossip would assign the windfall credit to her mother. However, she couldn't hide behind Roberta forever. Explaining how a widowed pastor's wife had purchased a house, no matter how small, wouldn't slip past Maxine.

Since their shared, and very public embarrassment, of getting high after accidentally eating pot brownies before the Christmas Eve service a year ago, Maxine had dropped her interest in renewing their old friendship. In fact, the board chairman's wife had returned to her hateful old tricks with a vengeance. Only this time, David and Amy's continued involvement with Angus and his vagrant friends had put them squarely in Maxine's sights. Leona may have agreed to step away from the parsonage and her former ministry obligations, but she wasn't about to give Maxine a reason to pull the trigger on David's ministry or his marriage.

Thus the need for a garage sale. One big enough to convince Maxine that Leona was scraping funds together.

"How much for all of these?" Angus Freestone held up J.D.'s herringbone tweed jacket. The lanky boy had filled out considerably since David had helped him move into his grandmother's apartment behind her diner, proof that eating at the Koffee Kup was as detrimental to one's waistline as Leona had long believed.

"Angus, why would you want these old suits?" Leona asked. "Wouldn't you rather have this little bookshelf? It's just the right size for a dorm room."

"No, ma'am." Angus slipped his arms into the jacket. "Reverend David says a person only gets one shot to make a good first impression." He grinned, extending his arms to check the fit. "And that's exactly what I'm fixin' to do."

Leona couldn't help but smile at how quickly Angus had picked up southern slang and at how close the bond had become between her son and Ruthie Crouch's grandson. Unlike Maddie, who'd made it abundantly clear her future did not include children, David was a natural when it came to kids. He would have made a terrific father.

Leona pushed the ache of never having grandchildren from her mind. God knew Amy's health issues when he chose her for David. From the happiness and contentment on her son's face, anyone with half a brain could tell Amy was *the one* for David ... diabetic limitations and all. As much as Leona would love to argue her son's case before the Lord, there were many things God had done over the last eighteen months that didn't make sense. Taking J.D. at his prime was first on her list.

"Exactly, who are you needing to impress, Angus?" Roxie asked.

"The scholarship committee at Abilene Christian University." Angus adjusted the jacket sleeves. "My counselor says I've got the test scores and the inspiring story. All I need now is a good haircut and a suit for the interview."

"Tell you what," Leona lifted the jacket off his shoulders. "Why don't you let me buy you a suit? One that fits properly."

"No, ma'am. The Harpers have already done more for me than I can ever repay." Angus lifted the other suits off the line. "This scholarship is somethin' I've got to earn on my own. I've been savin' my tips at the diner for these necessary expenditures." He pulled out a ten and two fives. "I think this is a fair price for the lot, don't you?"

"You drive a hard bargain, Angus Freestone." Leona took the worn bills from his hand. "Any college would be blessed to have you."

As she watched Angus tote the last of her dead husband's belongings down the sidewalk, a warm spring breeze brushed the top of Leona's head. J.D.'s kiss of approval, she thought to herself.

Roxie's elbow poked Leona's ribs. "Here comes your lawyer friend."

"Technically, he's J.D.'s attorney. And he's not my friend."

Roxie sighed. "That doesn't make him any less handsome."

Briefcase in hand and single purpose radiating from his set jaw, Saul Levy's march toward the parsonage was going to force him squarely into the path of Angus. The two had not spoken since Angus' accidental involvement with the pot in the Christmas brownies. Leona braced for the inevitable meeting and she could see Angus stiffen as well. To her surprise, Saul acknowledged Angus with a curt nod. Acknowledgement was progress, but it did not indicate full forgiveness. However, Leona took this tiny gesture as a sign Saul's wariness toward the boy was thawing.

Finally.

Since that fiasco, Angus had matured in mind, body, and spirit, thanks to the involvement of loving people like his grandmother Ruthie and David and Amy. It was way past the time for Saul to let his distrust go. Mentally shaking an accusing finger at him, she suddenly felt a finger of guilt pointing back at her.

She hadn't spoken to Saul, other than when business demanded, since she'd discovered he'd helped her husband with his secret legal affairs. Technically, Saul could make the point that she hadn't let go of her animosity, let alone her distrust.

Leona waved, trying to ignore the lump of hypocrisy creeping up her throat. "Hey, Saul."

The ex-JAG lawyer had long ago traded his military uniform for three-piece, well-fitted suits, but he was never without his aviator glasses. Leona couldn't get used to the idea of a man who dressed so intimidatingly formal during the week. "Suits are for Sunday," J.D. had always said, insisting his jeans and boots related to the locals. The size of J.D.'s funeral had proved his theory correct. Her rugged cowboy had indeed endeared himself to this West Texas community. Saul, on the other hand, wore his silk ties and crisp, French-cuffed shirts like a man dressed for white-collar warfare. His lack of charm wouldn't attract enough folks to surround his coffin for a decent graveside service.

Saul mounted the steps to the parsonage like he was late to a Pentagon briefing. His shiny shoes brought him to an abrupt, eye-to-eye halt directly in front of her and Roxie. "I have your papers, Mrs. Harper."

"Please, call me Leona," she insisted for the hundredth time.

"Leona." From his clipped tone, it sounded as if asking him to act as her legal representative in this small transaction had put him out.

She wished he would remove his sunglasses so she could get a better read on the truth. "Do I need to sign them now?"

Saul's head snapped toward Roxie. His brows rose above his glasses in what could be interpreted as his unwillingness to discuss Leona's business in front of anyone.

Roxie got the message. She lifted her chin. "I'll go tidy up the knickknack table." She sashayed just far enough away to make it appear she'd complied, but not so far that she couldn't shuffle picture frames and keep an ear tuned to their conversation.

Saul's jaw twitched in dissatisfaction, but when he saw that Leona wasn't going to offer to take their conversation inside, he set his briefcase on the large bedside stand Leona knew would not fit in her new home.

He cleared his throat. "Your son asked if he could look over the buyer's contract before you signed." He popped the brass latches on the case and removed a neat file. "Once David is satisfied everything is in order, come by and you can execute the closing papers in front of my notary."

The moment the file hit her hand, Leona forgot to breathe.

Pull yourself together, girl. It's just a house.

She squeezed the folder tight. "Juanita usually drops by whenever we need something notarized."

"That was before I bought the firm."

"Juanita loved to make house calls." Leona's attempt to nudge a smile from the lawyer fell flat. "I'll have David look this over. Thank you, Saul."

The man just stood there, legs apart, hands behind his back, as if awaiting permission to say more. While his stiff military stance was unnerving, it was her reflection she'd just noticed in his dark glasses that horrified her.

She looked awful. Even worse than she did the night Saul had physically carried her to bed because she was so high on Christmas pot brownies that she couldn't walk. As the humiliating memory overtook her, Leona let her eyes slide down the front of her t-shirt. Paint splatters, in various shades of parsonage beige, covered a faded Red River ski logo. Her hair was pulled back in a clip, and she hadn't bothered to putty over the dark circles under her eyes.

Tugging at her shirt hem, Leona knew that since Saul had never mentioned her disgraceful actions, he was too much of a gentleman to call out her unkempt appearance now. "Is there something else, Saul?"

He thrust out his hand in an unexpected gesture of friendship. "I wanted to wish you good luck, Leona."

She accepted his offer of a handshake. "I'm only moving across town."

"Change isn't always easy." Saul's grip was painfully strong. "But it is the only way forward."

Still angry that J.D.'s secret stock investments had forced her into bed, so to speak, with a man who only recently started attending her church, Leona pulled free. "I'll keep that in mind." She would trust Saul Levy with her finances, but not her personal struggles.

Without another word, Saul executed a well-heeled pivot and strode down the steps and back toward his well-ordered office.

"That was awkward." Roxie's touch jarred Leona from her stare glued to the lawyer's hasty retreat.

"Saul Levy is one tightly-wrapped package," Leona agreed.

"Maybe you should invite him to your dance class. A couple of good spins around the ballroom floor might loosen him up."

Leona gave Roxie a disgusted scoff. "That devil doesn't dance."

CHAPTER TWO

"I think that's the last of it, Parker." Leona held a towel in one hand and the knob to the lopsided screen door of her new home with the other. Rain pounded the small awning over the stoop and threatened to whip the door free of its broken hinges.

"Good thing y'all started after church. We just barely beat this toad strangler." The handsome county extension agent wrung water from his t-shirt. "Might even get enough rain to break the drought."

Leona held out the towel. "And send the weevils looking for higher ground."

"Which will lead to a bumper cucumber crop for the Story sisters, and you know what that means."

"More pickles," Leona laughed.

Parker refused the towel. "Wouldn't want to track mud on your new carpet, Mrs. H."

White carpet was a stupid choice, she knew. But it was her choice and she'd always wanted thick, snowy rugs.

"I'll rent a shampooer and let you push it, if it'll make you feel better." Leona pulled him in. "Since you won't let me put gas in your truck, you're gonna let me feed you. Amy's bringing pizza."

David poked his head out from behind a stack of boxes. "You know Momma's not going to let you leave hungry, right?"

"Guess I've got time to help you set up your electronics." Parker shucked his shoes at the door and came inside. His strapping 6'4" frame seemed to shrink the living room even smaller.

"Momma's right. We couldn't have done this move without you and your truck." David held out a ball of tangled electrical cords. "Want to tackle the TV or the computer?"

"The computer's a priority, if you don't mind, boys." Leona squeezed through the tight maze of boxes, painfully aware she should have let more stuff go. "Never know when Ivan might need me to work on an article from home."

Parker dried his hands on his pants. "Computer it is then, but after that I gotta scoot."

David dug the router and modem out of a box. "What's the

hurry, man?"

"I'm taking a Spanish class at the high school. We've got our final in a week."

"Spanish?" Leona ripped open the box marked PAPER GOODS. "I've always wanted to learn a foreign language."

Parker studied the knotted cords. "It's not too late."

"You're right, Parker." Leona pulled out a stack of paper plates. "I'm going to add Spanish to my bucket list."

"Right after dancing," David mumbled, his disapproval evident. "Momma's signed up for ballroom dancing lessons."

"Dancing?" Parker grinned. "Good for you, Mrs. H."

"First, a new house." David struggled with the new flat screen TV he was trying to lift out of the box. "Then dance lessons. What next, Momma? Skydiving?"

"Maybe." Leona flashed a tentative grin. She'd always wanted to take dancing lessons but J.D. had refused. He claimed they were already so in sync they didn't need professional help. But then he'd also claimed they were always flat broke. "I might even try snorkeling."

"You know you have to go near water to snorkel, right, Momma?"

Leona's stomached clenched at the thought. "Okay, traveling then."

Parker dropped the computer cords and rushed to David's

aid. "Nothing wrong with broadening your horizons." He held the T.V. box while David pulled on the screen. "I'm fixin' to do the same."

"You want to take dance lessons with me, Parker?" Leona asked. "Kendra Smoot has converted that deserted gas station and repair shop out on the highway into a studio."

"Didn't one of her kids fall in the old oil pit?" Parker asked.

"She has so many of them, she didn't even notice until bedtime," David teased.

"They've covered the pit, David," Leona said. "Since Kendra started her studio she's lost all her baby weight. Folks are driving for miles to take her tap, jazz—"

"Salsa?" Parker peeled the box from the TV. David staggered under the weight.

"I believe she does offer salsa," Leona couldn't contain her excitement at the possibility of snagging a partner.

"I might try to squeeze in a couple of salsa lessons," Parker grabbed one end of the TV, allowing David to shift to the other end. "I plan to tear it up at every village celebration when I move to Guatemala."

"Guatemala?" Leona and David said simultaneously.

Parker set his end of the TV on the antique dresser Leona had spent several days transforming with chalk paint. "Leaving in six months."

"Another mission trip?" David asked as he brought his end to rest on the dresser.

"No." Parker pulled the cords from the empty box. "I'm relocating. Permanently." Excitement radiated in his eyes. "Already put my ranch on the market and started training the new county extension replacement agent."

Leona felt her heart lurch. "Why Guatemala?" What she really wanted to ask was did Maddie know he was contemplating a massive lifestyle change? One that could forever put an end to Leona's hopes that once her daughter finished her residency she'd come home and realize Parker was the man for her.

"Last summer's mission trip cemented my plans." Parker unwound the twist tie around the cords. "There's a medical clinic down there in desperate need of repairs and the village where the clinic's located is struggling to access fresh water." He plugged the cord into the back of the TV. "They need an extension agent."

David clapped him on the back. "They couldn't get a better man."

"Is this the clinic where Maddie did a summer internship?" Leona asked as nonchalantly as she could.

Parker's cheeks flushed. "It is."

Leona sat on the stack of boxes. "Maddie loved that

place."

David shot her a daggered look that said *leave it alone, Momma*.

Parker plugged the cord into the wall. "I guess you could say it was Maddie's fault I fell in love with that place."

"Fell in love?" Leona asked despite David's finger slicing across his neck warning her to back off.

"I remember how radiant Maddie looked when she came home after spending the summer in those rugged mountains," Parker said. "She was on fire."

"Luckily it was just the flu and not some horrible tropical disease," Leona said.

"No, I meant, on fire for the Lord." Parker's eyes sparkled, adding to the impish charm that endeared him to everyone he met, everyone but Leona's daughter. "Maddie has always known what she wanted. But after spending a summer in Guatemala, she came home convinced," he said. "I wanted in on whatever it was that could give a person such a sense of purpose."

"Have you told her?" Leona asked. "I mean about your decision to move?"

"Tried, but busy medical residents must not answer their phones." Parker pushed the power on the TV and it flickered to life. "I can't wait around until she does." Disappointment flickered in his eyes for an instant. Then he quickly changed the subject to the short list of potential volunteer worship leaders he'd help train to take his place.

Saul was right. Moving on wasn't easy. At any age.

Later, after they'd finished eating pizza, Leona gave her favorite song leader her blessing. Then she watched as a diesel pickup carried her hopes of Maddie finding happiness into the rainy night.

CHAPTER THREE

"Morning, Leona," quipped the Mt. Hope Messenger's number one reporter without looking up from her computer.

"Morning, Modyne." Leona loved the smell of ink, pulp, and possibilities that hung in the air of a small town newspaper office. Digital news could never replace the touch of a human hand feeding the words through a press, or so she prayed.

Modyne continued to peck away on her keyboard. "Did the rain soak your mattress yesterday?"

There were worse things than ruined furniture. Letting a good man slip away from her daughter was one of them. "Parker had a tarp." Leona stopped at the desk of the grisly reporter who claimed she'd given up retirement because she hated living in a cramped RV with a man who snored. "Anything happen over the weekend?"

Truth was Modyne didn't like missing out. Leona had discovered an increased fear of missing out to be one of many hazards associated with the news business. Her sharpened senses had detected an underlying story in Parker's behavior. Had she not followed her gut and poked her nose into his business, she might not have learned about his Guatemala plans until it was too late. As it was, she'd have to work fast to implement Operation Unite Maddie and Parker. Six months was pushing it, especially when she considered how those two had circled each other for years without admitting how they felt about each other. But, she'd reminded herself as she'd pondered this predicament well into the night, David and Amy had fallen in love in a fraction of that time. All she needed was a reason to bring Maddie home. Immediately.

Modyne tilted her head toward the stack of messages on the corner of her desk. "Maxine wants you to do a background story on that new doctor."

"Dr. Calvert's been here two years."

Modyne peered over her glasses, her fingers still flying over the keyboard. "Like I said…new."

She needed something bigger than Maxine's dislike of their local doctor to pry Maddie away from her residency commitments for a few days. "Maxine doesn't want background. She wants dirt." She wadded up Maxine's message. "I'm not aiding and abetting that woman's campaign to run a perfectly competent doctor out of town simply because the man refuses to date her daughter."

The irony of those words pricked Leona's conscience. How was her plotting to run Maddie's life any different than Maxine plotting to run Nellie's? It wasn't and she should be ashamed. And she would be if it hadn't suddenly occurred to her that a potential opening at the hospital might be just the bait she needed. She mentally backpedaled. What was she thinking? She couldn't sabotage a man's career. Not even if it meant letting Maddie ruin her own.

Modyne raised her palms. "This ain't church, Leona. And you're not the pastor's wife anymore. You don't have to justify anything to anyone. Not even those silly dance lessons you've signed up for."

"I still need to be careful. This is a small town with big ears and bigger mouths. My boy can be hurt."

"David can fend for himself."

For now, David and Amy were on what was known in ministry circles as the honeymoon period. But their first year, when everyone believes the new pastor can do no wrong, was now behind them. It was only a matter of time before they could do nothing right. Whispered curiosity as to when David and Amy would start their family was already beginning to circulate. She hated to think of the sadness this would bring once it became evident that the answer was *never*.

"I hope you're right." Leona pushed her fears to the back of her mind, determined to break herself of the tendency to worry. "Come take dance lessons with me, Modyne."

Modyne waved her off. "The reporter beat has flattened my feet."

"I need a partner."

"RV living was my mid-life fling. Time for you to have yours."

"If you change your mind, the first lesson is Friday night."

"I'm free Friday night." The booming call of adventure startled Leona.

She hadn't heard this special voice in years, but instant recognition stirred so many wonderful memories. Leona whipped around to see a tall, sturdily-built man clad in a short-sleeved olive shirt, multi-pocketed vest, and khaki cargo pants. Sandy hair curled out from under a leather safari hat sitting rakishly-low across one side of his tanned face. Other than a few lines etched by too many years in the African sun, Roy McGee hadn't changed a bit.

"Roy?"

White teeth flashed in his pleased grin. "I've got moves smooth as a gazelle."

"And the subtlety of a bull in a china shop," she quipped.

"LeLe Harper." He opened his arms. "Beautiful and quick as ever."

No one but this man had ever gotten away with calling her such a silly nickname. Not even J.D. "Roy!" She ran to greet her friend.

Roy's strong arms scooped her up and swung her around.

Leona's head was swirling with questions by the time he set her feet back on the worn wooden planks. "What on earth are you doing in Mt. Hope?"

"Visiting my supporting churches." He held a steady grip on her shoulders, eyeing her with sincere appreciation. An appreciation she hadn't seen in a man's eyes since J.D. died, and hadn't realized she missed so much until now. "This time, I made sure Mt. Hope Community was first on my list."

"Why's that?" she asked, although she had a sinking feeling she already knew. Why hadn't it occurred to her to have a believable explanation handy? Of course, Roy would be curious as to why a small church that normally sent a paltry one hundred dollars a month would suddenly gift him ten thousand dollars.

"I think someone must have found oil on the church property," he teased.

"Why would you say that?"

"Howard was one of many of my supporters who sent me an email saying their church was unable to help pay my expenses to bring Ivy's body stateside after I lost her. So I buried her in Africa. Then, two years later, a sizeable deposit from Mt. Hope shows up in my bank account. I've got to get to the bottom of this miracle."

A change of subject suddenly seemed in order, especially since Leona could feel Modyne's eyes boring holes in her back. She shimmied free of Roy's grasp. "I'm sorry about Ivy."

Roy's cavalier smile slid, revealing a glimpse of raw pain. "I'm sorry about J.D."

A comforting current of understanding passed between them and aroused so many wonderful memories. While J.D. and Roy had been swamped with grad-school Greek, Leona and Ivy had busied themselves making ends meet on student loan budgets. She couldn't begin to count the times she and Ivy had combined their limited groceries to make a meal and share dreams. Since those long ago grad-school days, she and J.D. had gone on to serve two different churches while Roy and Ivy had traveled the world raising support for their main focus: a string of missions across South Africa. So many times she and J.D. had talked of going abroad for a visit, but they'd never been able to scrape together the funds.

"Are you hungry?" Leona asked.

Roy's smile crinkled the lines around his eyes. "If you're making chicken pot pie."

"I'll make you dinner while you're here, I promise. But I just moved into my own place and I couldn't find a stew pot right now if I had to. Come back at noon, and we'll go next door for a quick bite. I'll introduce you to my mission field."

"That's right." His eyes scanned the newspaper office. "You're a working woman now. I'm impressed."

"I've always worked, Roy. Just never got paid." She held up her finger. "Do not quote that eternal reward line you and J.D. used to toss at Ivy and me whenever we complained about another night of mystery-meat goulash."

"Those were good times, weren't they?" Roy chuckled.

Leona swallowed and whispered, "The best."

"David at the church?"

"For the first time in years, it's not my job to know who's in the church office."

Roy's big hand cupped her shoulder. "You can take the girl out of the parsonage, but you can't ever take the call of ministry out of the girl, LeLe."

Was that true? "You're welcome to drop by the church. Shirley will know David's schedule."

"I'll give your boy a shout-out, thank him for the financial support then swing by and pick you up for lunch. Sound good?"

Leona's heart skipped a beat. Not because she'd just made her first lunch date with a man who was not her husband, but because David didn't know about her contribution. It wouldn't take her son two seconds to trace the large sum back to her. She made a mental note to text David with a reminder to keep her money a secret.

"David has always enjoyed your adventure tales, Roy."

"And you?"

"Every time I hear your incredible stories, it makes me want to explore the world that much more."

He took her hand and brought it to his lips, his eyes capturing hers. "It's not too late." He tipped the brim of his hat and headed out the door.

Roy's kiss still sizzling on her hand, Leona turned.

Modyne was wearing her I-just-landed-a-front-page-story smile. "Old friend?"

Leona held up a palm. "This ain't church, remember?"

Noontime sunshine had heated the back of Leona's neck by the time Roy rapped on the newspaper window. She grabbed her purse and shoved away from her desk. "Heading out to lunch, Modyne."

"Might as well. You've been so starry-eyed, you haven't gotten a blame thing done."

She'd argue, but Modyne was right. Since seeing Roy, she'd only edited one obituary. The rest of her time had been wasted Googling passports. "Want me to bring you a sandwich?"

"I'm having leftovers." Modyne stopped pecking away at the computer. "I'd offer you some, but I can't see you ever settling for leftovers."

"I eat leftovers."

"Eatin' them is one thing," Modyne said. "Marrying them is another."

Feeling confused and a little undone by Modyne's comment, Leona stepped out to meet Roy on the sidewalk. He'd taken the time to freshen up. Bright white shirt. Khaki pants. A new straw safari hat. Roy McGee was nobody's leftovers.

"Get to see David?" She took Roy's offered arm, well aware that Modyne was watching through the glass. She was having lunch with an old friend, not walking down the aisle with him.

Roy patted the hand she'd threaded through his crooked elbow. "He's a fine boy, Leona."

"David is his father's son, that's for sure."

"I see more than a little bit of you in him, too."

How could someone as secure in themselves as David

possibly be anything like her?

"Roy McGee?" Maxine's voice jarred Leona from her ponderings. "We haven't seen you in a coon's age." Maxine and Howard stood outside the door of the Koffee Kup café.

Howard extended his hand. "Is it fundraising time again?"

Leona slowly extracted her arm from Roy's. "He's back for a little R&R, Howard."

Roy pumped Howard's hand like he was working one of the many water wells he'd dug in Africa. "I'm taking a six-month furlough on the dime of a very generous contributor."

"What do you mean?" Maxine asked.

"I know you fine folks would never flaunt the blessings the Lord has bestowed upon you,"—Roy winked at Maxine—"but just between us, there's no need to be so modest."

"I'm afraid I don't know what you're talking about, Roy," Howard said, sweat beads forming upon his bald head.

"Your gift of ten thousand," Roy explained. "That was you, right?"

"Ten thousand?" Maxine's eyes were so huge Leona knew they'd pop out if she told Maxine she'd written that check.

"Biggest single contribution my ministry has ever received. My accountant said the gift came from Mt. Hope. I just assumed …" Roy let his enthusiasm trail off

When Maxine realized someone in Mt. Hope had made

that contribution and it wasn't her, she let her eyes slide toward Howard. One glimpse of her husband's gaping mouth and she pretty much had her answer. The money hadn't come from him. That's when Maxine did the only thing Maxine could do … she covered her surprise with a scriptural reprimand. "Well, like you say, Roy. In matters of tithing, it's better if the left hand doesn't know what the right hand is doing." She tethered Howard with her arm. "We're in a bit of a hurry."

"LeLe and I were about to pop in for a burger," Roy said. "Why don't you join us?" Roy's invitation, while genuine, had the air of killing two birds with one stone. The man understood the importance of staying in good with supporters, even stingy ones like Howard and Maxine. "I'll be in town a few days and plan to use the time to catch up, with this sweet woman." His arm was an octopus tentacle wrapping Leona's shoulder.

"I know you and *LeLe* have a lot in common, both being recently widowed and all." Maxine's emphasis on Roy's pet name stung more than the recently widowed. "We wouldn't dream of intruding."

"Nonsense." Roy snugged Leona to him, with an over exuberance that told her Maxine's comment had left him smarting as well. "There's always room for others at our table, right LeLe?"

Maxine's brows rose. Leona wasn't sure if Maxine's

discomfort stemmed from the embarrassing nickname, Roy's public displays of affection, or the nasty prospect of sitting across the table from someone she hadn't had a civil conversation with in over a year.

Suddenly, the idea of investigating all three possibilities sounded extremely fun. Leona smiled and threaded her arm through Roy's and cozied close to his massive frame. "Absolutely, Roy."

"It's settled then." Roy pulled the diner door open. With a sweep of his hand, he ushered Maxine and Howard into the greasy world of fried meat and mashed potatoes. Angus, met them at the newly installed WAIT TO BE SEATED sign, his idea of making the diner into more of a restaurant, according to Ruthie.

"Hey, Mrs. Harper. Good to see you not eatin' alone." Angus, red hair slicked back and decked out in one of the suits he'd bought at Leona's garage sale, snatched four menus. "Y'all want a booth or a table?"

Seeing J.D.'s herringbone tweed filled with vibrant life had the unexpected effect of making Leona feel like a traitor. She slid her arm from Roy's. "A booth please, Angus." Leona followed J.D.'s jacket through the crowded diner. While she couldn't take her eyes off her husband's old jacket, she felt as if all eyes were on her. What was she doing having lunch with another man? And in such a public place? She never thought she'd be grateful for being forced to sit down with Maxine and Howard, but having them at the table was the buffer she needed.

"Leona?"

Leona stopped in front of the booth where Saul Levy sat having his usual burger, fries, and coffee. "Saul," she stuttered. "Uh, it's nice to see you."

Saul lowered his coffee cup. "I'm glad to see you're well, Mrs. Harper."

Leona's brow puzzled. "Well?"

The attorney looked from her to the man standing beside her. "When you missed your appointment this morning, I assumed you were ill."

Leona gasped. "I totally forgot." Yes, she had. The moment Roy walked in, all her other obligations flew right out of her head. "I can run by after lunch." She hated that she was babbling like a school girl. Saul was her lawyer, for Pete's sake, not her warden. "That is, if it's convenient for you."

"I've got a court appearance, but Juanita can give you what you need."

"This fellow a friend of yours, LeLe?" Without waiting for her introduction, Roy's hand shot in Saul's direction. "Roy McGee."

Saul wiped his mustache with his napkin, slid crisply from the bench, and stood. Feet apart, thumbs hooked in his belt loops, his power stance communicated no intention of reciprocating Roy's good will. "Saul Levy."

"Saul is my ... attorney." The designation hardly explained the man's rude behavior. Saul was what he was. So why did she feel the need to add, "Mr. Levy's helping settle J.D.'s affairs."

"I've always admired a legal mind." Roy let his unshaken hand drop. "And it's nice to have smart people around you in your time of need. That's why I'm looking forward to spending some quality time with LeLe. She's one sharp cookie."

Saul's eyes had returned to Leona. "A remarkable woman, indeed."

For once, Leona wished her lawyer's ridiculous dark glasses were covering his eyes rather than neatly tucked inside his shirt pocket. Saul's penetrating gaze made her feel as if she was standing in some sort of breath-sucking Bermuda Triangle: J.D.'s old suit brought to life behind her. A flamboyant old friend prodding her from the left. And her new uptight lawyer flanking her on the right.

Little beads of sweat morphed into trickles running down Leona's face.

"Leona?"

She could hear Saul calling to her. Tenderly, like he had that fateful Christmas Eve when her drug-induced stupor had forced Saul to carry her wasted body up the parsonage stairs. As futile as her efforts had been then, she couldn't make any part of her body respond to his command now.

"Have a seat, Leona." Saul's hand cupped her elbow and guided her to the bench he'd recently vacated.

"LeLe, you alright?" Roy asked, sliding in on the opposite side of the table. "Last time I saw you this pale, you'd just announced to J.D. that you were pregnant."

"I believe it's safe to assume she's *not* pregnant, Roy," Maxine snapped.

"Angus, bring Mrs. Harper some water." Saul's command was not to be argued with, by Angus or by her.

"It's just the heat," she told Saul, catching a strange expression on Maxine's face out of the corner of her eye. "I'm fine, really." Leona pushed out of the booth and offered Saul her hand. "I'd like to reschedule my appointment."

Saul's hand clutched hers. "Business can wait."

CHAPTER FOUR

"So Roy thought you were pregnant?" Roxie had not quit cackling about Leona's story. "I would have loved to have seen Maxine's face," she laughed as she pawed through one of the boxes of new bedding stacked in Leona's small bedroom.

"It was strange." Leona's head still throbbed with images from the whole embarrassing encounter.

Roxie ripped open the packaging on the new pillows for Leona's bed. "Strange that a man from your past suddenly appeared? Or strange because of Maxine's reaction to said man's interest in you?"

"Both."

"Maybe your gallant missionary has always had a crush on you and Maxine is jealous." Roxie tossed the pillows on

Leona's freshly made bed.

Leona caught a glimpse of herself in the dresser mirror. Hair in a clip, her favorite ugly paint shirt, and bags under her eyes. Even if she wanted to draw a man's attention, she was so out of practice she wouldn't know where to start. "Roxanne Brewer, you can put the brakes on those spinning wheels of yours right now."

"You didn't buy these nice new sheets so you can sleep alone for the rest of your life."

"The old ones reminded me too much of J.D. I needed a fresh start."

Her friend grabbed a bedpost and hopped up on the bed with an evil grin. "See what I mean?"

"I've got Tater." The dog lifted his head at the mention of his name. Once the aging cocker realized there was no treat in his future, he wearily laid his head on his paws.

"There's nothing fresh about that old dog." Roxie was right. Tater was nearly thirteen and, like his bedraggled mistress, beginning to show his age. She wouldn't have her furry companion forever. Then what? Roxie patted the bed indicating this conversation would go better if Leona would sit. "Obviously, something happened in that diner to upset you." Roxie was worse than Modyne when she smelled a story.

Leona pretended to tighten the new dresser knobs. Putting

her feelings into words seemed dangerously close to confessing her loneliness. She'd only spent one night alone in her new home. But it had been her first night alone in nearly thirty years. She'd expected quiet, but she hadn't expected the silence to be so painful. In the course of one night, she'd gone from feeling confident and courageous about her new life to terrified and impulsive.

Impulsive?

Yes, that was it. Impulses had buckled her knees in the diner. Standing between Saul and Roy, two very different men, neither even remotely close to measuring up to the man who used to wear the herringbone tweed, she'd felt this intense desire to run. Leave her loneliness behind. Seek her true purpose somewhere far away. And start over where no one had any preconceived notions of who she should or should not be. Crazy impulsive, right? Unlike her, impulsive. Worse than wearing red high heels to church impulsive.

Then the truth hit her. A hard punch to her gut. Moving out of the parsonage could have been a huge mistake. Perhaps her meltdown was the result of trying to stand on her own two feet before she was ready. If that was the case, she had no business thinking about men who could never fill this huge hole in her heart.

Roxie slid from the bed. "Leona?"

Leona jerked her unsettling emotions back into line. "Did you come to help me get settled or spy for my children?"

"I'm on your side, Leona." Roxie reached in a box and removed J.D.'s tackle box. "I see you decided to keep this."

Leona ran her hand over the cool metal. Each dent in the rusty box had been put there by her husband. "I sold his jon boat. His fishing poles. I couldn't let everything go." She set the empty box on the small table beside her bed. "You never know what you had until it's gone."

Roxie cocked her head, considering more than Leona's choice of placement. "You're going to need a shiplap accent wall if you're going rustic in here."

They both burst out laughing. Starting over was harder than Leona had ever dreamed and every bit as hard as Saul had implied. Good friends who understood the difficulty of each tiny step were a treasure. They were still laughing when the doorbell rang.

"I hope the Lord never asks me to do without you, Roxanne Brewer." Leona wiped tears of release from her face. "That's probably Saul with the final copy of my closing papers."

"You mean the ones you *forgot* to pick up because you were too busy thinking about a certain missionary?" Roxie's determination to move her on down the grief road had only stalled long enough for Leona to catch her breath.

"I mean, Saul said he'd drop them by. And that's all I mean." Leona ran to the living room, checked her hair in the mirror, then yanked open the front door. "Etta May. Nola Gay." Disappointment sounded in her welcome. "What brings you girls out this evening?"

Etta May thrust a jar of pickles at Leona. "Housewarming gift."

"Thank you." Leona took the jar and smiled at the silver-haired sweethearts grinning expectantly at her. While she hated to start a new precedent, one that might encourage the Story twins to show up on her new doorstep every Sunday morning, she couldn't very well take their pickles and not show them some hospitality. "Would you like to come in?"

Nola Gay shook her head and elbowed her sister. "Tell her the real reason we dropped by, Etta May."

"We're starting a business," Etta May crowed.

"A pickle delivery service?" Leona asked.

"No, pickles are our love offering to the Lord." Nola Gay took Leona's hand and pulled her out onto the stoop. "Look." She pointed to the large blue van parked at the end of the sidewalk. "We're tuber drivers."

"It's Uber, Nola Gay," Etta May corrected then whispered behind her hand to Leona, "Sister's been working with garden produce far too long."

"Uber drivers?" Leona repeated.

"You know," Nola Gay said. "It's like a taxi service."

"Only better," Etta May added.

"I know what an Uber driver is," Leona said, still processing how these two ancient relics had learned about such a modern service. "Maddie and I took an Uber last time I went to visit her in New York. I guess I'm surprised no one else in Mt. Hope seems to think we need Uber drivers here."

"That's exactly why we're gettin' in early," Nola Gay said. "Be first or go home, we always say."

"I've always had a terrible fear of pickin' up strangers," Etta May said. "Y'all remember how antsy I got when Angus passed out in the fellowship hall, him bein' a stranger and all," Etta May said. "But then Nola Gay pointed out we know everyone in Mt. Hope, including Angus now, so we'd only be drivin' friends."

"Or friends of friends, of course," Nola Gay added. "Come on, you've got to see how cozy our crocheted seat covers have made it inside." Before Leona could dispose of the pickles, Nola Gay pulled her down the sidewalk. "Howard Davis gave us a good deal on the van because it has nearly two hundred thousand miles on it." She kicked the back tire. "Howard was worried about selling it to us at first, but then I told him, 'We're 82, Howard. How many miles do you think we've got left in us anyway?'"

Etta May pulled a cell phone from her pocket. "We've even purchased one of these new-fangled phones, you know, the kind that isn't attached to the wall. I told Nola Gay we needed a pocket phone like we needed hemorrhoids, but she said we've got to be on call twenty-four-seven." She poked at the screen. "You want our new number, Leona?"

Leona could not let her imagination picture what it would be like letting two old women who had never worked a cell phone drive her around. Every Sunday morning, they parked on the curb outside the parsonage. No telling what they'd hit between their house and the Harpers. "I...well...I usually drive myself," Leona stuttered.

"I can understand your hesitation," Nola Gay said. "People say we should act our age, but we don't know what 82 should feel like. So we can act however we want, right?"

"The girl at the phone store told us all our clients have to do is type in their number and then I can type them a message and they'll have our number." Etta May held out the phone.

"You mean you'll text me?"

Etta May shrugged sheepishly. "Seems like it would just be easier to write it on a piece of paper, don't it?"

"Sometimes Etta May's slow to grasp progress," Nola Gay chided.

Etta May rolled her eyes. "We don't know for sure how this new business is going to work. Every time Nola Gay drives past a bathroom she has to stop. Can you imagine how long it will take us to get anywhere? But we thought, if Leona can step out in faith and buy herself a little house and build a new life, we can start a business."

"You're our inspiration, Leona," Nola Gay said. "We're proud of you."

She'd never been anyone's inspiration. "Thank you. That means a lot."

"Thank *you*." Nola Gay punched her sister's arm playfully, all bickering between them forgotten, whether by grace or true forgetfulness, who could say? "We need to finish our rounds."

Etta May climbed in the passenger seat and hollered out the lowered window. "Where we headin', Nola Gay?"

"I don't know." Nola Gay popped the van with a flattened palm. "But I'll see to it that we make good time." She gave Leona a hug then went around and heaved herself into the driver's seat.

They both were so excited that Leona didn't have the heart to throw water on their plan. Reservation bells ringing in her head, Leona typed in her cell number and passed the phone to Etta May. "Don't forget to text me so I'll have your number if I ever need a ride."

"That old van you drive ain't goin' to last forever, Leona." Nola Gay yelled from behind the wheel. "Why put more miles on your vehicle when you could ride with us?" She cranked the engine and pumped the gas. Black smoke belched from the tailpipe. Over the engine's roar, she shouted, "You give us a call, Leona. We'll be here lickety-split."

Etta May leaned out the window. "We'll give you the pastor's discount even though you're no longer a pastor's wife."

Leona clutched the quart of pickles as she watched the Story twins rattle off in their big blue van. She was so busy contemplating the new danger rolling down the streets of Mt. Hope that she didn't hear Saul's Lexus glide to a stop. Nor did she hear him get out of the car.

When he touched her elbow and asked, "What was that?" she dropped the pickle jar on the sidewalk.

Hopping back from the shattered glass and sticky-sweet juice, Leona gasped, "You scared the pickles out of me, Saul."

He looked at the mess and chuckled. "Are you hurt?"

She didn't know Saul Levy knew how to smile. That he was smiling at her was even more surprising. "You think this mess is funny?"

"Not the mess," he smiled. "Your assessment of the mess."

"My assessment?"

"I didn't know it was possible to *scare the pickles* out of someone," he continued to chuckle like it was the funniest phrase he'd ever heard.

"Oh." Leona wiped her hands on her shirt. J.D. had never laughed at her jokes. He was the funny one. "It's either laugh or cry, right? And crying has never changed a thing." She bent and started picking up the bigger pieces of glass. "The Story twins dropped off a housewarming gift in their new Uber van." Before Saul could say anything, she added, "Don't ask."

"Let me help." He tucked the large manila envelope he was holding under his arm. In the blaze of a West Texas sunset, this man who was never without a starched shirt or a military crease in his dress slacks, started sorting glass and pickles. "Maybe you should get a bag to put this in."

"Right." Leona's moist fingertips trailed the crusty dried paint stains splashed across her shirt. Oh. My. Goodness. She was a mess. Again. "I'll be right back." She dashed into the house, calling for Roxie. "I need a trash bag. And a makeover."

"What on earth?" Roxie bolted from the bedroom, a lampshade in hand.

"Too long to explain," Leona shot to the kitchen and ripped

through the PAPER GOODS box. "Lipstick. I need lipstick."

"You packed your makeup with the paper towels?"

"No! I need yours. Now!" Leona snatched a plastic bag from the box, pleased that at least something in her life was as organized as her attorney.

Roxie raced to her purse and pulled out a sleek tube of burnt amber. "This shade is totally wrong for your coloring."

"I don't care." Leona peeked into the glass on the microwave door and smeared rusty brown across her lips. Without taking time to blot, she grabbed the trash bag and shot out the front door. "I found one."

Saul, who was still squatted in the middle of scattered pickles, started laughing. Quietly at first, like he was trying to control himself, and then full out laughing. A belly laugh that shook him from the top of his high and tight haircut to the soles of his shiny shoes. A laugh, Leona found surprisingly attractive. "You looked like a bat on fire flying down those steps."

Relieved he wasn't commenting on the jaggedness of her quick lipstick fix, she said, "You'd be surprised what I can do with a trash bag, Saul Levy." Leona pursed her lips in an effort to even the color and threw the black bag around her shoulders. Around she went, stopping after turning a 360, then jammed her fisted hands on her hips like she was some sort of superhero.

"No, I don't think I would." He stood, his eyes locking with hers. "You've done more with far less than any woman I've ever known."

He'd noticed. Surprise deflated Leona's stiffened shoulders. All those years of scrimping and saving and barely getting by and she'd thought no one cared. She stood there, draped in plastic, reveling in the fact that her sacrifice had been duly noted and, from the admiration in Saul's eyes, appreciated. Heat flushed her face. "Thanks."

Saul nodded toward the bag she wore, indicating he needed a place to dump the stack of glass he balanced in his hands. Leona removed her trash bag cape. As Saul dropped in the broken shards, his hand brushed hers. Intense warmth surged through her body and loosened rusty emotions she'd screwed down years ago.

Hot flashes, she reasoned. What else could it be? "I can get a broom for the rest. Clean it up later."

"We've about got it." Saul bent and scooped up a pile of pickles "You know, I've been thinking, you could have built a mansion on the lake, bought any house in this town, including the parsonage, and yet you chose a fixer-upper in a modest neighbor." His head tilted in the direction of her small brick ranch in need of lots of work. "I suspect by the time you work your magic, this house will be every bit the showplace you've made the parsonage." He dropped the pickles in the bag.

Magic. He thought her capable of magic. "Or it could be lipstick on a pig."

"Excuse me."

"A southern saying for an investment that may not be sound." She pointed at the large envelope tucked under his arm. "Is that for me?"

"It is." He looked at his sticky hands and then at the package. "Mind if I wash up before I hand it off?"

"Sooner or later you're going to get tired of cleaning up Harper messes." Leona pulled the ties on the trash bag. "This way."

Saul double-timed his steps, cutting off her retreat into the house with his solid body. "Leona, you're not making a mess of anything, least of all J.D.'s investments."

J.D.'s money had become more of a burden than a blessing. Until now, she'd never considered how nice it was to have someone who knew the full weight she carried. "Really?"

"Really. In fact, you've grown your husband's portfolio considerably and I suspect by the time you've finished with this property, it will have appreciated as well." Approval leapt from his gaze and got snagged on a need she thought she'd buried.

She was her own woman now. The only one she needed to please was God. But having a man she was growing to respect professionally pleased with her abilities was intoxicating. "Who knew all those years of stretching a dime into a dollar would prepare me to handle millions?"

Saul's smile lifted his mustache. "God."

"God has some explaining to do." She carried the trash bag up the steps. "Don't expect much. It's only my second night away from home...I mean," she stopped and turned. "I don't know why I said that."

"The parsonage may belong to the church, but the home you made in that house will always belong to you."

Sentiment from a man she considered to be a junk-yard dog? The thought unsettled her nearly as much as learning her husband had kept secrets from her.

"If you're not careful, Saul Levy, someone might find out a heart beats beneath that stiff shirt." Leona pulled the handle on the screen door and the frame came loose in her hands.

Saul lunged and caught the screen door before it crash down on her. The envelope fell to the stoop. "You alright?"

Nose to nose, their faces separated only by rusty screen, they stood immobile. Both were breathing hard, more from the surprise of the door's collapse than the fact that Saul's sticky hands were securely clamped over hers, Leona told herself.

Her sputtering pulse short-circuited all the half-way sensible things she should have said. "Saved me twice in one night," tumbled out of her mouth, as disorganized and unkempt as her appearance.

Saul released her immediately and took a step back. "One of the dangers of my job."

"Don't think you'll have to save me forever."

"I don't."

The way he said it, so self-assured and certain, fit his personality. What didn't add up was his certainty in her, a certainty that had eluded her at every step of this new journey.

Hands shaking, Leona leaned the broken door against the house. "Come on in. If you dare."

CHAPTER FIVE

In the corner of Leona's tight little galley kitchen, her best china sparkled on the small round table she'd ordered from one of those online discount sites. Roxie had stayed until well past midnight to help with the assembly of all the pieces, including the two tall stools. She'd always thought those little bistro sets were so cute, but J.D. had made it clear he didn't want to eat towering over his food. Besides, he always said, they had a perfectly good dining set. Why would they want to spend the money?

Why indeed? Had J.D. penny pinched so she'd have to deal with the millions after his death? It would have been so much easier if she'd died first.

Leona crammed the bag of extra furniture screws in a drawer. She'd double-checked the table's directions several times and couldn't figure out why they'd had so many screws and washers left over. She'd still be going over every joint if Roxie hadn't pointed out that this second-guessing herself had to stop, if she was to have any hope of enjoying a fine meal with a fine man.

Water plunked into the sink. Leona cranked the faucet lever and the knob came off in her hand. Something else to fix. She jammed the knob back onto the rusty bolt. The drip would have to wait.

She wiped her hands and peered through the glass of her new oven for the tenth time. To her relief, the chicken was roasting on schedule. She didn't know what she'd been thinking when she decided to throw this impromptu dinner party. Working with an untested oven was asking for trouble. Anything could go wrong. The sleek appliance could heat too hot. Heat too slow. Ruin her hurried prep in an instant. Then what would she do? Call the Story sisters, and ask if their Uber service delivered pizza? Did her male guest even eat pizza?

"Who doesn't eat pizza?" Leona muttered to herself as she wiped her hands on her apron and opened the door to her matching stainless steel fridge. Two perfectly tossed salads waited on one of the shiny glass shelves. Cold air swirled around her as she stared at how little she had to offer. Pizza and salad. Not much of a backup plan if her dinner failed. With a nervous sigh, she closed the fridge door. Having nothing to serve was the least of her worries.

She may have invited the wrong man.

The doorbell rang. Tater shot from the kitchen and raced for the front door. Leona ripped the apron over her head, smoothed her hair while glancing at her reflection in the microwave glass, then took a deep breath. It was just dinner with a friend, she told herself. She took a deep breath and turned the knob.

"David? Amy?" Leona hadn't meant to let her disappointment sound in her voice. She didn't want to have to explain why her first dinner invitation in her new home had not been to her family.

That wasn't it.

She didn't want to tell her son she'd invited a man. Which was crazy.

Leona had mentally replayed the uncomfortable conversation at their last family gathering at least a million times. Before the turkey was cold, Maddie brought up the subject of Leona remarrying. She and David had obviously discussed the possibility behind her back. Each presented a list of reasons as to why their father would not have wanted her to grow old alone. Both had been adamant about her moving on.

Or so they said.

Leona knew from her experience with her own mother that saying you're ready for your single parent to explore another relationship was one thing. The reality of your parent remarrying was quite another. Although Leona couldn't be happier with her mother's decision to elope with Cotton, it had taken time for her to get over someone taking her father's place. David and Maddie deserved all the time she could give them.

"Smells like Thanksgiving in here," David came in without waiting to be invited.

Leona shuffled her body between David and his view of the china laid out on her kitchen table. "I'm baking chicken."

Amy's beautiful blue eyes took in the living room. "Everything looks so beautifully…settled. How did you do it?"

Leona expected Amy to be pleased she was out from under foot, not impressed she'd accomplished so much in so little time. "Roxie's worked me like a Hebrew slave."

David's long legs carried him to the couch in three smooth strides. Before she could say *don't get comfortable*, David said, "You look extra nice this evening, Momma."

Leona smoothed her new red skirt. "Just got home from work."

Which was true, but her nosy son didn't have to know that she'd flown out of the newspaper office at exactly five o'clock, whipped into the grocery store, grabbed two chicken breasts, took the shortcut home, tossed the chicken in the oven, sprinted to her closet, ripped the tags off the new outfit she was wearing, and touched up her hair and lipstick.

"Work all day." David's hand showcased the living room. "Unpack boxes every night. And still have the energy to cook a homemade meal." David didn't smell chicken. He smelled a rat. He wasn't buying her story.

"I'm not decrepit." Leona straightened a lamp shade.

David draped his arms across the back of her new gray linen couch. He definitely wasn't leaving until he got to the bottom of this. "I told Amy, I'll bet you Momma will be moving back into the parsonage with thirty-six hours."

"Did you now?" Leona had never owned anything linen. It was all she could do not to tell her son to be as careful about where he put his oily hands as he should be with his assessment of her will.

Amy went and sat by her husband. "And I told David, when his Momma sets her mind to something, you better get out of her way."

Pleased at Amy's definite shift to her camp, Leona perched on the edge of her new swivel club chair. She crossed her legs, then uncrossed them quickly. Her new red heels weren't even scuffed on the bottom. Luckily, David and Amy were so distracted by whatever it was that had brought them here, they hadn't seemed to notice her new shoes.

Just why were they so distracted? "What's going on?" Leona asked.

"Can't a son drop in and check on his widowed mother?"

"You've done that several times this week." Leona eyed them carefully. "Something's up. You're glowing. Both of you."

"Are we?" Amy's eyes twinkled.

Suddenly the cause of Amy's uncharacteristic moodiness became apparent. Leona's heart stopped. "Oh. My. Goodness. You're pregnant, aren't you?"

Their heads bobbed excitedly, grins big as dinner plates breaking across their faces.

"But ..." Leona's muscles tensed and her defenses rose. What were they thinking? Her shaky hand flew to her lips and stopped the lecture forming on her tongue. She couldn't ruin this moment of happiness. They knew the risks. This moment of happiness could be very brief and they deserved every second.

Amy was a private person. Leona had worked long and hard to gain her daughter-in-law's trust. Giving their relationship room was one of the reasons Leona had decided to move out of the parsonage. Amy, like all young brides, needed breathing room. As Leona watched Amy's nervous hands caress her flat belly she knew it had taken everything within this precious girl to share the news that they'd gone against doctor's orders.

"We just came from another sonogram," David's tone was a little defensive, as if he'd read her mind. "Everything looks good."

"Another sonogram? How far along are you, dear?"

"Almost eighteen weeks," Amy could see how keeping something this important a secret had stung. "I was afraid to tell anyone until we were well past the first-trimester mark."

Bad case scenarios ripped through Leona's head so fast she could barely nod.

"Amy's sugar is under control," David said, irrepressible hope glowing in his eyes. "The doctors feel confident *we* can do this."

"We've got a long way to go." Amy's locked hands formed a shield across her womb. This girl was willing to do whatever it took to protect this little life, even if it meant risking her own. "So we've come to ask for prayers."

"Of course." Leona opened her arms and swallowed her terrified children in a hug. "I'm so happy." And she was. New life. A sign from God that they *could* all go on. "Your father would have been thrilled," she told David. "And your parents would have been over the moon, Amy."

"We're not ready to tell anyone yet, Momma," David warned.

"Have you told Maddie?" The moment Leona blurted out the question she knew the answer. It was written all over David and Amy's guilty faces. "Of course you have." Leona released their hands and took a step back.

Her children had kept secrets from her, and they'd done it while she was living under the same roof. David and Maddie were definitely cut from their father's bolt of cloth.

"When Amy and I started to seriously consider expanding our family, we both felt we should put adoption on hold until we fully investigated the risks of having our own child. We needed ..." David let his words trail off.

Unwilling to hide her hurt, Leona said, "A *medical* opinion?"

David shifted uncomfortably. "Momma, we know how you are. We didn't want to get your hopes up."

"So you talked to Maddie?"

"She said Amy needed three months of optimized glycemic control, folic acid supplements, and a complete workup from a maternal-fetal medicine specialist before we dared to proceed to conception."

Preferring not to dwell on the nuts and bolts of how this baby came into being, Leona focused on the inconvenient details. "Is that why you've made so many trips to the city?"

David nodded. "We don't have the specialists or facilities Amy needs in Mt. Hope."

All the motives she'd assigned to David and Amy's behavior had been wrong. They weren't ignoring her, and they weren't trying to squeeze her out of the parsonage. They were two scared kids trying to weigh the pros and cons of a very difficult decision.

"Aren't you worried the stress the trips could place on—"

"There's lots to worry about, Momma," David interrupted. "That's why we're not ready to tell anyone yet."

The three of them sat there, no one speaking, everyone remembering how painful it was to listen to the well-meaning condolences of the congregation after J.D.'s death. David was right. The loss of a baby would be hard enough on them. Having to explain their loss again and again would be more than anyone should have to bear.

"This is your news to tell whenever you believe the time is right," Leona assured them. "But it's mine to treasure ... forever."

The doorbell rang.

Leona froze.

Her children and her late husband weren't the only ones who could keep secrets. And this one was a doozy. She'd forgotten all about her date. What a blow it would be to David and Amy if they found out this way.

Now what?

"Momma?" David tapped her hand. "Want me to get the door?"

"No!" Leona ran her sweaty palms down the front of her skirt and stood. She put on her company smile. "Would y'all like to stay for dinner?"

David and Amy traded glances.

"Sure," David said.

"Great. Stay right there." Leona hurried to the door. Through the glass, she could see Roy waiting on the bottom step, a big bouquet of flowers in one hand and a beautifully wrapped package in the other. She threw the door open. "Roy, so good of you to come."

"Whoa. You're prettier than an African sunset." His eyes twinkled. "Red is definitely your color."

Did he mean the flush heating her cheeks or just red in general? "Thanks."

"Twirl around, and let me look at you."

"That's silly, Roy." Leona was shaking her head, but he kept on insisting. "Okay." She stepped out onto the stoop, looked both ways to make sure none of her neighbors were watching, then took a quick spin. The breeze twirled the skirt's silky fabric around her knees and for a moment she could almost feel herself dancing.

Roy released a pleased sigh. "You're more beautiful than I remember, LeLe." He thrust the flowers at her. "Sorry I'm late. I've lived on African time for so long, I may never get used to the American obsession with promptness."

"No worries, Roy." She held the beautiful assortment of blossoms to her nose and drew in the heady scents. "We're not on the clock tonight."

Roy rewarded her with that killer smile of his and a deep and pleased inhalation of the evening air. "Is that chicken pot pie I smell?"

"I'm afraid I didn't have time for that recipe. Hope roasted chicken breasts will do."

"Guess I'll have to settle for the company then." He winked.

She fingered one of the soft rose petals. It had been years since anyone had given her flowers. J.D. would have, but she'd shut him down claiming the money could be better spent. What other pleasures had her overly cautious ways cost her? Why had she lived when J.D. was the one who obviously had so much more to live for?

Roy leaned in and caught her eye. "LeLe? We eating outside tonight?"

His question snapped her from the survivor's guilt. "I'm sorry." She indicated he should follow her and turned for the door. "Let's get these in some water."

Roy stepped inside and snagged her arm. "Wait, LeLe." He handed her the box, a mischievous look in his eye. "I seem to remember a woman who couldn't get enough of these."

Leona drew the box to her chest. "Please tell me this box is stuffed with dried mangos."

"To the brim." Roy's arm hooked her waist and reeled her in so tight Leona felt the cardboard flatten inside the wrapping paper. He smelled of leather and sunshine and life. His lips gently brushed against her forehead. Heavenly feelings coursed through her body. Sensations she hadn't felt since the Sunday J.D. nuzzled her neck right before they left the parsonage for what would be his last sermon.

"Uh, Momma?" David's voice gave them both a start.

She and Roy broke apart, each taking a step back and flushing red like two junior high campers caught kissing behind a tree.

"Roy," Leona stuttered, the flattened box of mangos still pressed to her chest. "I hope you don't mind, but I've invited David and his wife Amy to join us."

Roy's smile went stiff. "I always love jawing with your boy, LeLe."

David's eyes cut to Leona's. She was certain he hadn't missed the red creeping up her neck any more than he'd missed the intimate way Roy tossed her nickname around. "Truth is, Roy, Amy's been on her feet all day and she's worn out." David turned to Leona. "If you don't mind, Momma, I think I'll take my wife home."

"If you're sure." Leona held Roy's gifts like a shield to her chest.

"We're sure," Amy winked.

If she had any hope of fixing her bumble onto the dating scene, it had to be now, before David got on the phone and called his sister. "Roy, I'll just see them off, if you don't mind." Leona thrust the flowers and mangos at her speechless guest. "Make yourself at home." She followed David and Amy to their car.

"I didn't know you loved mangos, Momma." David opened Amy's door.

"There's lots you don't know about me."

"Apparently. Roy McGee is a … surprise."

"Don't make a big deal out of this. Your father and I knew Roy and Ivy back in grad school. He's a recently widowed missionary *friend* on furlough and I'm …"

"A beautiful woman," David kissed her cheek. "Remember, not a word about me and Amy to your *friend*."

"God is the only one who'll be hearing from me about you, *if*," she paused for emphasis. "...Maddie won't be hearing about me from you."

David was silent for a moment. "Deal."

Leona nearly skipped up the sidewalk. When she stepped back inside Roy had made himself at home. He'd put her flowers in a vase, set her crushed package on the coffee table, and was standing by the fireplace looking at the family pictures.

"J.D. was quite the guy."

Leona sucked air through the hole her heart. "Yes, he was."

She'd spent the last two days putting Roy off, claiming she needed time to put her new home together. Now, that he was here, she wished she hadn't wasted precious moments. "How long are you staying in Mt. Hope?"

"Now that depends." A flirtatious smirk lifted the corner of his mouth.

"On what?"

"On whether or not you've already found a dance partner."

"I have not."

"How many weeks do these dance lessons last?"

"Six."

"Then that's how long I'm staying."

She smiled. "Really?"

"Only a fool would turn down the opportunity to learn to dance with a beauty like you." He scooped her up. "Wait until you see what these two left feet can do." Effortlessly, he spun her around. Leona burst out laughing. She was still laughing when he set her red shoes on the white carpet, his hands tight on her waist.

She was still giggling when he kissed her, on the mouth this time. The feel of his lips on hers was a pleasure she'd missed more than she knew possible. Slowly her hands raised and wrapped his neck. And just like riding a bike, she was kissing him back. Their connection only lasted for a few seconds, but an eternity of possibilities skyrocketed in Leona's head.

He pulled away gently, leaving her breathless. "I've wanted to do that since the first time I saw you."

Leona's breath caught. Her mind raced backward. Surely Roy hadn't meant he'd wanted to kiss her that long-ago Sunday morning when she and J.D. first bumped into Roy and Ivy in the church potluck line? "You mean since you surprised me at the newspaper office, right?"

Roy didn't immediately discern that he'd been

misunderstood, but when her uneasiness finally dawned on him, he flushed. "I loved Ivy with all my heart. I miss her."

The only detail Leona knew of Ivy's death was that a horrible fever had taken her in a few days. It must be the shared experience of the sudden death of a spouse drawing her to Roy, because she had no intention of ever putting herself in the position of losing someone she cared for again. However, spending time with someone, who'd been blindsided as painfully as she, did have an undeniable appeal.

She silenced him with a finger to his lips. "As I miss J.D."

Roy slipped his hands into his pockets and took a step back. "You have a screwdriver handy?"

"What?"

"Your screen door is off its hinges. Want me to hang it?"

Laughter exploded from a place so deep she could feel emotions nailed firmly in place break loose. This was the first really good laugh she'd had since ... she couldn't even remember the last time. "Roy McGee, you are a true romantic."

"Wait until you see what I can do with your leaky kitchen faucet."

"I've learned I don't need a man to take care of me."

He gave a nonchalant shrug. "Just want to earn my dinner."

"That's all?"

His clear blue eyes were an ocean inviting her to jump in. "You know it's not, LeLe."

"You'll find J.D.'s tools in the garage."

"I kept Ivy's mixing bowls." Roy's gaze locked with hers. "Don't know the first thing about how to use them, but just couldn't let them go."

While Roy hung her door, Leona bustled around the kitchen thinking about what else Roy hoped to earn. Her companionship? Her trust? Her heart? She could feel his appreciative eyes watching her through the screen. Intense heat flashed from her core. Her snug new outfit made no allowances for the building steam to escape. She pried open the window above the sink and sucked in the cooling evening air. She'd been out of the romance business for years. Quite possibly she'd read more into Roy's proclamations than he'd meant.

She'd gotten used to handling repairs herself, and had even begun to enjoy the freedom that came with making her own decisions. But, if she was being honest, she also missed the sound of a man fixing things.

For years, J.D. had been her repairman. He could replace a drippy faucet, stop a drippy car radiator, or soothe her drippy tears. Whatever mess life threw at them, her husband had always helped her sort it out and right the wrongs. And he did it armed with little more than a hammer and his great sense of humor. Sorting the mess J.D's death had made of her life had been one of the hardest parts of being on her own.

Or so she thought, until Roy McGee swept her into his arms.

Hoping the heat from the new oven was the cause of the perspiration on her lip and not her own foolish ponderings, she was grateful when the stove timer finally went off. She lit the candles on the table, dabbed the moisture from her lips, then went to the entry where Roy was tightening the last screw on the screen. "Pretty handy with tools aren't you, mister?"

Roy smiled broadly. "Never knew what to expect when I was in the bush." He opened and closed the screen a few times. He stepped inside. The door closed snugly without as much as a squeak. "Truck might break down. Pump go out on a water well. Or a lion could have ripped through a hut." Adventure oozed from his pores, its scent as intoxicating as the flirtatious twinkle in his eyes.

She reached for the screwdriver from his hand. "Come, tell me about Africa."

His free hand caught hers. He slowly drew her fingers to

his lips and brushed a kiss across her knuckles. "Come with me and see it for yourself, LeLe."

CHAPTER SIX

Roy's captivating stories of water wells dug, reed homes built, and churches planted had lasted late into the night. Leona had been so deeply affected by Roy's tales of all the lives he'd changed, she couldn't quit thinking about his offer to take her to Africa. If she didn't have to fly over water to get there, she might have left with him on the first plane out of Dallas.

Leona sipped her coffee, hoping the caffeine would chase away the sleep-deprivation grogginess as she waited in Saul's favorite booth. Although she'd taken a page from Roxie's book and dressed like a woman intent on getting things done, she needed more than a flattering blue suit and taupe heels to sway Saul Levy. She needed a clear head. One important key element had to be put into place before she could give serious consideration to Roy's proposal to follow him around the world.

She stared at the open menu, her stomach in such a knot she didn't really have an appetite.

"I thought our meeting was set for seven." Saul stood beside the booth, a frown on his face, as he checked the watch on his wrist. "It's only zero sixty-thirty hours."

It took a second for her tired, civilian mind to convert his military-time reporting. "You're early then."

"Thirty minutes early *is* on time in my book."

She smiled and invited him to sit. "Mine too, actually."

He removed a plainly wrapped brown-paper package that was tucked under his arm, laid it on the table, and slid into the booth. "Have you ordered?"

She stared at the package. "Just coffee."

Saul made no effort to explain the package. Was it for her or just something he happened to have with him? Instead, he held up his finger and Angus sauntered over with a steaming coffee carafe and an empty cup dangling from his thumb.

"Morning, Mr. Levy," Angus said cautiously. Saul simply nodded. It was still winter between them. "Miss Leona," Angus's smile pleaded for her help.

"Morning, Angus." Leona shoved her drained cup his direction. She never would get used to seeing J.D.'s herringbone tweed every time she came in the diner for a bite to eat. But she believed in this boy, and she'd forgiven Angus for his involvement in the pot incident. Hopefully, Saul would follow her lead. "How'd your scholarship interview go?"

Worry knotted Angus's brow. "I haven't heard anything."

She patted his hand. "You will."

Angus tugged proudly at his jacket. "Until then, I'm dressing for success." He set the coffee pot on the table and pulled a notepad out of his pocket. "Havin' the usual this morning, Mr. Levy?"

"Yes," Saul didn't waste time on words and neither should she. If this meeting went as planned, he would officially become her legal counsel. His billing by the hour would most likely include today's breakfast conference.

She closed the menu. "I'll have what Mr. Levy is having."

"Want your eggs scrambled or fried?" Angus asked Leona.

"However Mr. Levy likes them is fine with me."

Angus got the hint that she was in a hurry and left them to their business.

"That boy deserves to go to school," Leona told Saul as she watched him meticulously tear the top off a sugar packet and empty the contents into his coffee. "I want to help if he doesn't get that scholarship."

Saul stirred his coffee with one hand and slowly eased the brown package toward her with the other. "Read this first."

So the package was for her. A gesture of kindness she was not expecting. "What is this?"

"A housewarming gift."

"You didn't have to do that." She lifted the package and undid the simple course string. The paper fell away and revealed a hardcover book. "The Intelligent Investor?" She didn't know whether to be offended or impressed he believed her capable of tackling a brick-sized volume on money management. "Not your usual coffee-table-kind-of-book."

"It's not for display." Saul laid his spoon on a napkin. "It's for your benefit."

"I thought you said I was doing a good job managing J.D.'s investments."

"You are."

"Soooo ... why do I need this?"

"Everyone can profit from direction."

"I'll cherish it, I'm sure." She slid the book under her purse, wondering what had happened to the easy banter they'd experienced over a broken jar of pickles. "Speaking of business, I'm anxious to get on with ours."

Saul raised his cup and took a sip. "I'm listening."

"I know you're acting legal counsel for the hospital." Pleased to show off her research skills, she waited to play her next card. Saul's steely stare didn't confirm her knowledge of his clientele one way or the other. Left with no choice, she played her ace. "I'd like to invest in the future of Mt. Hope's little medical facility."

"Invest?"

"Increase the services and medical care they currently offer to the residents of our rural county."

"Specifically?" His eyes drilled her over his cup.

A few more details to support her position might be in order. Fortunately, she'd done her homework in the medical stats as well. "Diabetes rates are high in our largely rural county, especially among the poor. Medical care availability and quality are on the lower spectrum. Seriously ill patients must either drive to Dallas, Lubbock, or Amarillo."

"I'm well aware of the burden."

Was he? How? Why? Refusing to allow herself to be distracted, she tabled her questions and went in for the kill. "I want to change those odds."

"How?"'

"Hire a maternal-fetal specialist."

The slight stiffening of his posture was her only clue that he'd not seen this one coming. "Convincing the hospital to take on such an expense won't be nearly as difficult as trying to convince a specialist to come to a sub-standard hospital with a less-than-desirable financial incentive of assisting the uninsured."

Grateful that Maddie had warned her there would be impediments to her plan, she was ready for this argument as well. "Then we'll have to sweeten the offer."

"I'm listening."

"First, we offer a very generous and competitive salary. Second, we pay off all of said specialist's medical school debt. Third, we allow said specialist to direct the remodel of the existing unused hospital space in order to best accommodate a practice of this sort. Fourth, not only would such a renovation raise the hospital's standards, it would increase our community's prominence in West Texas. People would drive to Mt. Hope for their medical needs and while they're here, they'll spend money."

"I'm assuming you intend to fund this monumental endeavor."

"I do."

Saul lowered his cup slowly and looked her dead in the eye. "So you *are* pregnant?"

"What?" She stiffened. "No." It wasn't until she noticed the smug satisfaction twitching beneath his mustache that she realized he'd actually made a joke. "You're teasing?"

"You're not the only one who can be funny."

No one had ever thought her funny. Odd thing was, what

she'd just proposed was not intended to be funny in any way, shape, or form. Determined not to let this man get under her skin, Leona clasped her hands and leaned forward. Careful to make sure no one in the diner was within listening distance, she whispered, "J.D.'s attorney-client privilege extends to me now, right?"

Following suit, Saul leaned in as if they were on some sort of clandestine mission and whispered, "If I was your attorney, then yes, that privilege would extend to you. But other than helping with your house closing, as it stands, you've made it clear that I'm *only* your friend."

Friend? That was a generous assessment of their interactions. "I'd like you to be more than a friend, Saul."

His eyebrows rose.

Before he could respond, Leona jumped in to clarify. "I mean, I'd like to hire you as *my* attorney."

He leaned back in the booth and crossed his arms, his willingness to play along over. "What does your son think about this?"

"David's far too busy at the church to be bothered with my legal concerns." Leona wrapped both hands around her coffee cup. "And he's about to get even busier."

"You're a grown woman. Capable of hiring whomever you please."

She was, and she smiled generously to show her appreciation of his recognition. "Do we need to sign something or can we shake on our arrangement?" She offered her hand across the table.

His hand met hers over steaming coffee. "You can send my retainer check later." His grip was decisive, sure, and strangely comforting. That he did not let go unsettled all the progress they'd made. "So, tell me, Leona, why do you want the hospital to have a high-risk specialist on staff?"

She pulled free, wiping the unexpected clamminess from her palm on the napkin in her lap. "I have my reasons." The heat from his touch would not be so easily rubbed off.

"And they are?" Saul waited while Angus slid steaming plates of eggs and bacon, along with the check in front of them. "Leona, I can't help you if I don't know the whole story."

Her glance bounced from the check to the crowd in the diner.

Angus and Ruthie were busy brewing fresh coffee. Four old men in the opposite corner booth were too deep into their political discussion to care about what she had to say. Most of the other regulars hadn't made it in yet. Attorney-client privilege or no, she'd promised David she wouldn't tell their precious secret. She directed her gaze back to Saul. His unwavering eyes communicated his unwillingness to allow his surroundings to pressure him to behave one way or the other. He was who he was. A silent man whose non-judgmental expression radiated trust and safekeeping.

Leona sucked a deep breath through her nose and leaned in close. "My daughter-in-law is … pregnant." The moment the whispered words left her mouth, Leona realized she was relieved to have someone in whom she could confide. Comfortable as she'd felt with Roy, she hadn't shared at this level with him, even when he'd pried a bit after David and Amy's hasty exit.

Saul's eyes softened. "You'll make an excellent grandmother."

She could tell his compliment was as sincere as his belief in her ability to manage J.D.'s investments. Which was good, since what she was about to ask him would require faith in her judgment. "Thank you, Saul." She and J.D. had dreamed of grandchildren. But if she was going to accomplish her mission today, she couldn't allow her mind to focus on the prospect of experiencing this next phase of life alone. "Amy's pregnancy is also considered high risk."

"I see."

"Amy must receive the absolute best care available. Right now, she's forced to drive three hours into the city. During her last trimester, I'm afraid that kind of grueling trip will become far too exhausting."

"I can understand your concern, but there are a couple of serious flaws to your plan that must be addressed before we proceed."

What was it about this man? One minute they were on the same side. The next, they weren't. "And they are?"

"Acquiring hospital privileges requires the physician to undergo an extensive credentialing process. Even if we could hire your specialist today, I'm not certain the hospital could complete the time-consuming process before Amy's delivery, let alone provide the care she'll need during the last trimester."

She hated being told no. "Mt. Hope's hospital is small. It's not like the powers that be are tied-up vetting dozens of doctors. I'm sure the process could be temporarily circumvented, or at least expedited."

He gave a doubtful shrug.

Feeling her mother bear urge to protect her young coming out of hibernation, Leona growled, "And the second flaw?"

"Isn't hiring Amy's doctor overstepping your boundaries?"

"What do you mean?"

"You told me that one of the reasons you were moving out of the parsonage was so that David and Amy could have a little space. Make their own decisions."

She'd expected a lecture on the risk of liquidating stocks, not to have her own words thrown back at her. Who did Saul Levy think he was commenting on how she should manage her family? As far as she knew, he didn't have children. Besides, he worked for her. Not the other way around. "Providing my daughter-in-law with excellent medical care is not the same as trying to tell her how to be a good pastor's wife."

"So why would you dare try to tell Amy how to be a good mother?"

Leona reared back as if he'd slapped her. "I'm not."

"Hiring her doctor basically says you don't think she has the ability to manage her health or the health of her child."

"Are you going to help me or not?"

He crossed his arms. "I think there might be more prudent ways to spend your money, and your efforts."

"And you want me to *pay* you for that advice?"

"That's how an attorney-client relationship works."

"You know what?" Leona grabbed her purse and book, fiery retorts blazing on her tongue. "They're my children. It's my money. And I'll spend my efforts and my money however I want." She wriggled out of the booth and dug out her wallet. "Who knows I might even go to Africa." She yanked a twenty from her rainy-day stash. "You're not the only lawyer in town.

I'm not about to make a man rich who thinks I'm a meddling, addlebrained busybody." She slapped the wrinkled bill on the table. "Send me an itemized statement for the hours you've spent settling J.D.'s affairs, drawing up my closing papers, and for this useless session, and I'll send you a severance check."

"It'll be in the mail this afternoon." He waved the twenty at her. "Breakfast is on me."

"I don't ever want to owe you anything, Saul Levy." She wheeled and stormed from the diner.

CHAPTER SEVEN

"Could there be a more irritating man on the planet?" Leona ripped open the UPS box. Flesh-colored dance shoes fell to the bedroom floor. "That arrogant little short rib dispensed advice like he was Dave Ramsey and James Dobson rolled into one."

Roxie examined the investment book Leona should have thrown in her attorney's face, and would have if she hadn't been so distracted by the fire in his baby blue eyes. "Saul dispensed advice because that's what you'd hired him to do."

Leona snatched up her new shoes, the ones the dance instructor claimed were great for beginners, would last for years, and were as durable as they were practical. "Well, he's fired now." She plopped on the bed and jammed a foot into one of the satin pumps with the force of Cinderella's ugly stepsister.

"I think you should have given him a raise." Roxie put the book on the nightstand, right beside J.D's tackle box. "The last thing our struggling little hospital needs is a massive renovation."

"Since when do you turn your nose up at progress?"

"Since I've seen our business drop off by fifty percent."

Leona sat up, her gut aching. "I didn't know."

"We've weathered worse. We'll weather this."

"Maybe this town wouldn't be dying if people had a reason to come here. And besides ..." Leona bit her tongue.

"Just as I thought,"—Roxie wagged her finger.—"you've got an ulterior motive."

She'd promised David she wouldn't tell anyone about the baby. She'd broken that promise by telling Saul their secret, which to her terror, might technically no longer be covered by attorney-client privilege. Roxie knew her deepest secrets, including how wealthy she was, but it would break David's heart if she told Roxie about *his* baby. So she lowered her head to concentrate on the straps and buckles on her shoes and finished up with, "Besides, Saul Levy and I are simply too incompatible to make it work."

Roxie held Leona's navy dance skirt to her own waist and twirled side to side in front of the full-length mirror. "You don't have to be compatible with the man … unless you're planning to marry him."

Leona's head snapped up. "I told you, I'm never going to remarry."

"So why have you spent an hour on your hair and a hundred dollars on this chiffon skirt?" Roxie waved the filmy fabric like a Matador cape, daring Leona to charge through.

Leona snatched the skirt from Roxie's hands. "Roy's a friend." She pulled the skirt over her dance leotard and spun the fitted waistband around until the silky bow draped her left side.

"People marry their friends," Roxie held out the tube of lipstick Leona had picked up on her way home from work, a rich pink concoction the teenage clerk said flattered her coloring. "They don't become enemies until they've had a couple of kids and several financial setbacks."

The doorbell rang.

"That's Roy." Leona snatched the lipstick.

"I'll entertain him," Roxie purred as she shoved Leona toward the mirror. "You go ahead and put on the finishing touches to your princess costume."

Leona barely recognized the woman staring back at her. Hair swept. Fitted leotard. Flimsy skirt. Hopeful eyes. "Maybe I shouldn't go."

Roxie came and stood behind her, placing both hands on Leona's shoulders. "Maybe you should stop breathing. If you were actually dead, you wouldn't have to feel guilty anymore for being alive." She kissed the sting of her words from Leona's cheek. "Hell's bells, Leona. It's time you returned to the land of the living." Roxie sashayed out the door.

Leona sunk onto the corner of her new bed, a bed she'd never shared with J.D. What had she been thinking? The man who could replace her husband did not exist. Which was just as well since she had no intention of filling the vacancy.

Ever.

She bent and fastened the shoes' thin straps over her arches. She'd expected to feel like Cinderella tonight. Instead, her hands shook so badly she could hardly manipulate the tiny buckles.

Unlike the infuriating Saul Levy, Roy McGee was a friend.

Handsome and charming. True.

A dance partner for this lonely time in her life. True.

Nothing more. True.

Or was it?

She drew the luscious pink across her aching lips, lips that had not been kissed in almost two years before she'd paid for Roy to ride into town. Is that why she'd sent him money? Had she secretly wanted Roy to come for her? Maybe Roxie and her children were right. Maybe it was time for her to move on with her life. Find someone to make her laugh again. Who cared where he came from or how he got here?

Muffled voices traveled the hall and hovered outside her bedroom door. Roxie's and ... she listened more carefully. The other voice was not Roy's magnanimous tenor. Leona scowled and plastered her ear to the door.

She jumped back. *What is Maxine doing here?* Leona smoothed her skirt, checked her hair one last time, then dashed to the living room.

The lanky woman who hadn't forgiven her for...everything wrong in her life...sat in Leona's new club chair, her face buried in her hands, violent sobs wracking her body.

"Maxine, what's wrong?" Leona's confused gaze flew to Roxie.

Roxie's hands raised in surrender. "I swear, I didn't touch her."

Memories of the day Maxine's teenage son died flashed in Leona's mind. She hurried to Maxine's side and dropped to one knee. "Maxine." She dared to touch Maxine's shoulder. "Has something happened to Cornelia?"

Maxine could only manage a slight shake of her head.

Leona looked to Roxie. "Would you fix her some coffee? Three creamer packets and two Sweet'N Lows."

Roxie nodded and ducked into the kitchen.

"Maxine?" Leona took the quivering hand of the wife of the chairman of Mt. Hope Community Church's board. "Talk to me."

Maxine raised her head. Mascara streaked her face. "It's Howard."

"Has he been hurt?"

"Not yet." A new wave of tears surged down Maxine's cheeks.

Leona's brow scrunched in confusion. "Maxine, that doesn't make any sense."

"I'm going to kill him," she blubbered. "Hurt him as bad as he's hurt me."

"Maxine, I need you to start at the beginning."

"Pssst." Roxie motioned for Leona to join her in the kitchen.

Leona shook her head, unwilling to leave Maxine.

"Now," Roxie mouthed.

Leona patted Maxine's knee. "I'll be right back."

Once Leona reached the kitchen, Roxie pulled her aside and whispered, "I think Maxine caught Howard with his hand in the cookie jar, if you know what I mean?"

"I have no idea what you mean, Roxie."

Roxie pulled her even closer. "For some time now, rumors

have been circulating through the auto business."

"What kind of rumors?"

"It's possible that the Cadillac dealer has…traded in his old wife for a newer model."

"Howard's having an affair?" came out louder than Leona intended.

Roxie put her finger to her lip, her eyes wide. "What else could it be?" she whispered.

"Lots of things," Leona defended. "Howard's chairman of our elder board. He's one of Mt. Hope's largest contributors. He's—"

"Not a saint." Roxie cut her off. "No one is, Leona."

The church hadn't dealt with anything this scandalous since Deacon Hornbuckle ran off with his blonde secretary years ago.

"Who's he seeing?" Leona asked.

Roxie shrugged. Her gossip had limits, even if she and Maxine had never been friends.

For that, Leona loved Roxie even more. "I'll take it from here." She grabbed Roxie's arm and drew her close. "Not a word of this to anyone."

"Goes without sayin'." Roxie slipped out the back door.

Leona took a deep breath and snatched the paper towels from the holder. She braced for the ugly truth, praying Roxie was wrong. She tiptoed into the living room and perched on the edge of the coffee table. Knee to knee, she sat opposite the bawling woman. "Maxine." She waited for Maxine to grab a breath then she lifted her chin. "I can't help you if you don't tell me what's going on." She cringed at how strangely reminiscent her opening line sounded just like Saul's.

"It's…your…fault, Leona," Maxine sobbed, snatching the offered paper towel from Leona's hand.

"What's my fault?" Although Maxine had blamed Leona for everything wrong with the world since the day her son Colt died, it would be helpful if she got specific. "Tell me."

"After Howard and I had lunch with you and Roy," she snuffed. "I got to wondering who'd given Roy all that money. Maybe Howard had done it and didn't want me to know. Which was so unlike him. The husband I know has always loved getting the credit for anything good. But the past couple of years, he's become extra secretive and super defensive every time I ask him any questions about our finances. I started to worry that maybe the Cadillac dealership was in trouble."

"Financial stress can be hard on a man," Leona agreed, hoping to keep the conversation moving.

"So can a prickly wife." Self-judgment ran deep in Maxine's eyes. "And I've been prickly for far too long." She blew her nose in a crumpled paper towel. "I did something I'm not proud of, but I did it just the same."

"All of us have done things we're not proud of, Maxine," Leona confessed.

"I mean what I did is way worse than wearing gaudy red heels to church, Leona." Even in her grief, Maxine could still deliver a stinging jab. "I waited until Howard left for work today, then I called one of those computer geeks to come help me break the passcode on his computer."

"You hacked Howard's personal computer?"

"And his work computer," she admitted. "My husband has been secretly withdrawing nearly five thousand dollars a month from our joint account. Do you know what he's been doing with our money?"

"Charity work?"

"Men call those kinds of withdrawals charity work when some lucky woman is calling him her sugar daddy." She noticed Leona's confused expression. "You're gonna make me say it, aren't you?"

"Say what, Maxine?"

"Howard has a mistress, Leona. There. I said it. Are you happy now?"

Leona's stomach dropped. "Oh, Maxine." She reached for Maxine's hand. "I'm so sorry. Maybe it's not what you think."

"What else could it be? He's paying another woman's rent. I know it." Maxine pulled away, her face contorted with pain. "I don't want your *sympathy*, Leona." She swiped her tears with the back of her hand. "I want *your attorney* to take my case."

"Maxine that might—"

"I know I don't deserve your help, not after how I've acted since the pot brownie incident, but I don't know what else to do. Howard will hire some highfalutin' city lawyer and leave me with nothing. I need a lawyer who'll clean his clock and teach him a lesson." The pleading tone in her voice was a knife to Leona's heart.

Leona worked to swallow the sticky mess she'd made when she fired her attorney. "You want me to ask Saul to be your divorce lawyer?"

"Yes."

"Have you tried talking to Howard? Letting him explain?"

"No." Maxine was resolute in her rejection of that idea. "He doesn't know I know, and I don't want him finding out from you or that Brewer woman. Where is she, by the way?"

"Roxie is the soul of discretion," Leona assured her.

Maxine chewed on her bottom lip, weighing her options. "Will you ask Saul Levy to help me or not?"

Becoming a party to the end of a marriage made her stomach sick. "What if you and Howard tried some counseling first?"

"And give Howard time to hide more money? I think not."

An energetic rat-a-tat-tat on the screen rattled Leona from the mire of Maxine's crumbling marriage and her failed relationship with one of the best lawyers in town.

Roy! Lord, she'd forgotten all about her date with Roy.

Leona glanced at the clock. *And on time! Why did he pick tonight to give up his African ways?*

"We'll think of something, Maxine." Leona held her breath, hoping Roy would think she wasn't home and decide to meet her at the dance studio.

Rat-a-tat-tat. Rat-a-tat-tat.

Maxine dabbed her eyes. "You goin' to get that or not, Leona?"

Leona let out a pained sigh and hurried across the living room, hoping to intercept Roy on the stoop and keep him safely out of sight.

But the moment she opened the door, Roy burst in, flowers in hand and a huge smile on his face. "Ta-da!" He spun around on the balls of red and black dance shoes. Her date had shed his standard safari attire for flowy black pants, a tight-fitting black shirt with enough buttons left undone to expose a few chest hairs. He had a new black fedora with a small red feather cocked on the side of his head. "Ready to give 'er a whirl, beautiful?"

"Roy?" Maxine took in Roy's appearance, her mouth hanging speechless.

"Roy," Leona's voice squeaked. "Could you wait outside?"

To her surprise, Roy instantly assessed that the source of Leona's angst was Maxine's troubled state. Looking more like a debt collector for the Mafia than an African missionary fresh from the bush, Roy set out to prove he could still charm the gristle off a pork chop.

He swept across the living room and presented Maxine with the bouquet. "For you, madam." His arm came across his trim middle and he took a deep and graceful bow.

Maxine brightened for a moment at the male attention. Then, as if she needed Leona's approval, Maxine's let her gaze hop from Roy to Leona. And that's when, for the first time, the wronged elder's wife noticed what Leona was wearing. Maxine burst into tears. "I've obviously interrupted your evening, Leona." Flowers clutched to her chest, Maxine picked up her handbag and bolted for the door. "Forgive me."

"There's nothing to forgive, Maxine." Leona followed her down the stoop. "It's not what you think. I promise. We're just taking dance lessons together."

Maxine stopped and turned. "Most of us will never get a second chance." Her anger had been replaced by a haunted expression, a loss Leona understood by heart. "Dance, Leona, and don't look back."

CHAPTER EIGHT

Before Roy could ask what had sent Maxine packing, Leona grabbed a couple of bottles of water and suggested that they get on the road. She needed a moment to process Maxine and Howard's dilemma.

Roy didn't needle her with questions, which she appreciated. Instead, he whistled some tune she didn't recognize and helped her navigate the step into his shiny, 4-wheel drive rental jeep as if the start of their date had been everything he'd hoped. He closed her door and nearly waltzed around to the driver's seat.

How much of her money had he spent on impressing her with this expensive ride? The question was a dagger to her conscience. "Where did you get the car?"

What was she thinking assigning expectations and motives

to how someone used her gift? A gift was a gift. When had she become like Howard and Maxine? Giving with strings attached rather than giving for the pure joy of sharing her blessings?

"Howard let me pick a car off his lot to use while I'm in town." Roy cranked the engine.

"Maybe Howard was feeling unusually charitable." Leona couldn't get Maxine's wounded, tear-streaked face out of mind.

"Howard's always been good to me." Roy backed down the drive. "I know he says he didn't send the money for my trip home, but who else could have done it?"

"Who else indeed?"

The dissolution of Howard and Maxine's marriage would devastate more than just the Davis family. Before Leona came into her millions, the Davises were the largest contributors at Mt. Hope Community Church. Since David took the pulpit, the congregation's morale and attendance had improved. But the town's economy was not recovering and the weekly contributions had remained stagnant. If it weren't for Howard's occasional infusions of cash, Mt. Hope Community would have shut its doors a year ago.

Leona had carefully considered her options. She could use her wealth to help fix the expanding shortfall, or she could let the weekly total, the one reported in the bulletin and posted on the wooden board on the stage, remain low, except for the months Howard kicked in extra. In the end, she'd chosen to avoid causing a sudden spike, knowing an increase of that magnitude would set tongues to wagging and send curious minds digging deep to locate the source of the increase. For now, she preferred to keep her wealth a secret. She'd been careful to funnel her tithes into special projects. A new youth van. Camp scholarships. And the all-expenses-paid furlough of the handsome grieving missionary escorting her to her first dance lesson.

"Maxine seemed upset." Roy wheeled his jeep onto Main Street. "Anything I can do?"

Was there anything anyone could do? She knew the work required to piece marriages together. J.D. had invested hours and hours into the couples he'd counseled. Sometimes it worked. Most times, it didn't. Why? Because once someone made the decision to jump the fence, driving them back to the barn was almost impossible.

"Pray," she said softly.

"Keeping my biggest contributors happy is always high on my prayer list."

"I hate the business of ministry."

"Water wells don't dig themselves, LeLe. Unfortunately, it

takes money to make a difference in the world." Roy reached over and squeezed her knee. "That, and an adventurous spirit." Hope raised his eyebrows until they disappeared beneath the brim of his black fedora. "Given any more thought to comin' with me to Africa?"

Seeing Maxine's marriage fall apart had obliterated her anger at J.D for not telling her about his stock investments. When J.D. made his little expenditures, he probably thought they wouldn't amount to anything. Spending a bit of money without telling her was small in comparison to Howard breaking Maxine's heart. J.D. had loved her and she still loved him. What she'd had with J.D. would never be duplicated. She'd been a fool to allow the possibility to sweep her off her feet.

"Could we just dance tonight, Roy?"

He gave her a brief, side-ways study then flashed a charming smile. "I didn't spend $39.95 on this flashy get-up to miss out on an opportunity to hold you in my arms."

Leona chuckled. Roy's easy manner was as close to J.D. as she would ever come. Yet something held her back and she knew what it was. Roy McGee was not and never would be J.D. Harper. "You really can charm gristle off a pork chop, Roy."

His brow furrowed at her valiant attempt to make him

laugh. "What?"

"It was silly. Never mind." She pointed to the old gas station up ahead on the left. Neon lights bathed a gravel lot filled with vehicles. "That's the studio."

"Guess I can have your oil checked after I give you a few spins around the dance floor," Roy laughed at his own joke as he wheeled the jeep off the highway. He idled slowly down the line of pickup trucks until he found a parking space in a darkened corner. "Are you sure you didn't sign us up for square dancing? 'Cause all I see are ranch vehicles."

Leona pointed to the lighted sign she'd passed a dozen times before she'd gotten up enough nerve to call.

BALLROOM LESSONS EVERY FRIDAY NIGHT.

"Starlight and satin slippers it is then, pretty lady." He hopped out, raced around to her door, and flung it open. He reached in and took her by the waist. "Ready?"

Suddenly her stomach felt as undone as the day J.D. convinced her to strap herself into the harness of a rickety zipline in the Hill Country. "Give me a minute, will you, Roy?"

"Second thoughts?"

"No," she said out loud, more to bolster her own confidence than to satisfy Roy.

"'Cause if you're wanting to back out, we don't have to do this."

"I thought you had moves like a gazelle."

"I did thirty years ago." His scrunched face and honest confession reminded her of J.D. when he stretched the truth for the sake of a laugh. "But unless dancing is like riding a bike, I may be too old to start over."

Was she too old to start over? If so, what was she doing here with Roy? Had she agreed to partner with him because hanging around Roy felt like taking up where she and J.D. had left off? "Let's hope dancing is like riding a bike."

He tucked a stray hair behind her ear then gently stroked her cheek. "You're as beautiful as the Serengeti in spring." Admiration gleaming in his eyes, he leaned in and kissed her. The tender brush of his lips was a feather duster lightly removing a layer of grief. "Let me show you Africa."

"Roy," she said, as she breathlessly pushed away. "I thought we'd agreed tonight we're just here to dance."

"I don't know about you, but my heart *is* dancing." With a wickedly pleased grin, he offered his hand and helped her navigate the descent from the jeep's running board.

Her own heart racing, Leona freed her hand and picked her way across the gravel lot, walking on the balls of her new dance shoes. Music boomed from every crack in the gas station's newly painted stucco.

Maybe she'd been a bit hasty in deciding her future.

Maybe happiness didn't have to look exactly as it had with J.D.

Roy slipped his hand in hers. "Nervous?"

If the Lord wanted her to have a second chance at happiness, maybe tonight was her shot. "I've never danced with anyone but J.D. And he had two left feet."

The lights in the parking lot illuminated the devilish twinkle in Roy's eye. "Keeps the bar low for me, then." He leaned in and kissed her. Again.

CHAPTER NINE

Leona's heart was doing all sorts of unusual gyrations after Roy's series of kisses. Either she was too old to take up flirting again, or she was on the verge of suffering a heart attack of her own. What would happen once she attempted real physical exertion was only one of her worries. What if she let her heart open toward another man? No, she couldn't. The strain of it would kill her. And she wasn't about to let herself die before setting foot on the dance floor.

She peeled out of Roy's arms. Maybe if she forced her mind to consider all the sober issues pressing her, the giddy cartwheeling in her stomach would settle down.

David and Amy and their baby. No, thinking about that scary situation would send her elevated blood pressure through the roof. Especially since there wasn't a thing she could do about obtaining the proper medical care Amy needed.

Parker leaving the country. Maddie was too busy getting her career off the ground to realize how close she was to letting a fine man slip through her fingers. Saul's warning immediately pricked a hole in this dark cloud. She hated to admit it, but that arrogant attorney was right. If she continued to butt in on her children's lives, she'd run the risk of alienating them. Then who would be the lonely one? Besides, she hadn't come up with a good reason to bring Maddie home, let alone worked out the details of how she'd throw her daughter and Parker together before he left town.

Okay, there was Maxine's crumbling marriage. That was a dreadfully sad situation, and she didn't want to feel sad tonight. She'd had enough sadness to last her a lifetime. Maxine hadn't gotten herself into this mess overnight. Helping her sort this mess out would take more than a single Friday evening.

Other than the thought of spending the rest of her own life alone, she'd come to the end of her list of serious matters. For now, she had no choice but to embrace the excitement of Roy's offered possibilities.

She turned to her handsome dance partner and took his hand. His approving wink set her heart soaring. She floated into the studio in a swirl of navy chiffon and crashed smack into a brick wall masquerading as Saul Levy.

"Are you alright, Leona?" Saul, serious faced as ever, steadied her with a firm grip on each of her arms. While he'd shed his business suit, he'd exchanged it for a monkey suit consisting of a white tuxedo shirt, white bow tie, black vest, and fitted black trousers that kept his rigid posture perfectly aligned. The only thing about his appearance that indicated he'd come to the studio for fun, was the pair of shiny black dancing shoes peeking from beneath the crisp hem of his pants.

Of course, she wasn't alright. Her son's wife needed a good local doctor. Her daughter was throwing away her chance at love. Her concern for Maxine made her feel guilty for running off to have a good time. Roy McGee was turning her world upside down with kisses and promises of exotic travel. And just when she thought the night couldn't get any more awkward, she'd just body-slammed the lawyer she'd fired at breakfast.

The last thing she wanted to do was demonstrate her lack of coordination in front of a man who was looking at her like he was presiding over a court-martial rather than pleased that they'd inadvertently signed up for the same fun-filled evening of dancing.

Leona pulled out of Saul's grasp. "I thought you didn't dance," she shouted over the beat of loud music.

"I didn't say I didn't dance," Saul's grin carried a tinge of smugness. "I said, I preferred not to."

Did he mean with her? "You don't owe me an explanation."

"You're right. I don't." He nodded toward the young Smoot woman standing in the middle of the ballroom and clapping her hands in an attempt to gain everyone's attention. For a girl who'd had five kids in six years, the petite brunette was fit and trim and full of energy. "Kendra is a client. Lessons were part of her retainer."

Leona smoothed her skirt, fully aware that Saul's explanation was directed at her horrible accusations. The possibility of Saul charging her huge fees was not the reason he'd helped her and she knew it. Saul Levy was an honorable man who would never gouge anyone, and she was a hothead who'd acted shamefully.

Heat crept up Leona's neck. "Kendra can be quite persuasive when she spots a potential client."

"Unlike me?" he asked, implying she'd dug herself into a deeper hole.

Before she could redeem what little was left of her pride, Roy interrupted. "Saul." Roy's offered hand was met by Saul's dismissive nod.

"I believe the class is coming to order." Saul executed a military-pivot and marched to the opposite side of the four-car repair bay now a single dance room. He settled into the empty space next to Ruthie.

Ruthie?

Leona did a double-take. The gray-haired diner owner had poured herself into a silver-sequined top and a mid-calf, flowy skirt. Ruthie flashed a broad smile and waved to Leona, then slipped her hand through Saul's proffered arm. Shock froze Leona in place. Were Saul and Ruthie a couple? Ruthie was at least ten years older than Saul. Maybe fifteen. What was he thinking? The woman did cook the man three meals a day. She'd seen men do far more for far less.

Roy nudged her with the elbow of his crooked arm. "Shall we give it a whirl, LeLe?"

Stomach clenching, Leona slipped her arm through Roy's. "That's why we're here." Together, they stepped out onto the wooden planks.

The air was thick with the scent of new paint, spandex, hairspray, styling gel, and excitement. Leona's eyes scanned the group. While she recognized most of the faces, and was certain most of Kendra's patrons recognized her, Leona was relieved that except for Saul and Ruthie, none of the other dance students attended Mt. Hope Community Church.

Leona's heels clicked past Kendra visiting with two elderly dancers as she and Roy walked toward the only space left along the mirrored wall opposite the garage doors. The slot next to Saul and Ruthie. With each step, Leona could feel Saul's eyes raking her over. If only Kendra had not had the oil changing pits securely covered. She could have dropped in, broken her neck, and have been spared the need to make civil conversation with a certain lawyer.

Far too soon, she found herself sandwiched between Saul and Roy. Heart thumping to the rapid beat of the music, Leona kept her eyes focused on the instructor, averting her gaze from Saul as if he didn't exist. All she could do was pray Kendra would realize that allowing two blue hairs to tie her up in conversation was impinging on everyone's dance time.

Just as Leona's heart was about to beat out of her chest, Kendra gave the nervous couple a reassuring pat then sprinted over to the boom box and stopped the music.

The lithe instructor picked up a microphone and waltzed out to the center of the now quiet room. "Welcome to the first night of the rest of your life." The young woman nearly glowed at the sight of her growing business. "I believe it's never too late to learn to dance." Uncomfortable jitters kept everyone's eyes focused on their instructor. Only two couples out of the ten were younger than Leona and Roy. "I truly believe anyone can learn to dance."

Leona hoped Kendra's pep talk applied to repressed ex-pastor's wives. She'd long admired the older actors who appeared on *Dancing with the Stars*. Especially those who'd never had a dance lesson. They had to know they couldn't compete against the younger, more athletic contestants. And yet, in spite of their obvious disadvantage, they tapped their courage, donned their sparkly outfits, and threw caution to the wind.

Maybe love the second time around was like being on *Dancing with the Stars* later in life. Leona cut a sideways glance at Roy. He was a good man. Filled with a holy zeal to serve the Lord. Life with an adventure seeker would never be dull. Leona let her hand drift Roy's direction. He twined his fingers through hers. A warm tingle raced up her arm.

"Let's start by talking about your shoes," Kendra said. "I hope y'all took to heart the information I emailed when you signed up."

Leona did what everyone else did and glanced at her feet. Her beautiful satin pumps looked exactly like the picture attached to Kendra's email. She'd even ordered the same nude color so her shoes would go with anything. Relieved she'd done something right tonight, Leona straightened her shoulders and stood a little taller.

"Dance shoes are strange and marvelous things," Kendra continued. "They're like magic. Their grip can hold you in place when you need to be steadied. Or the specifically designed sole can slide when you need to move. A proper shoe can greatly enhance your safety, comfort, and enjoyment as you maneuver the boards." She held up an old dance shoe. "Your shoes are like a good marriage. They should feel firm on your feet, but not so tight as to rub a blister."

Suddenly Roy's grip felt as if it had climbed Leona's arm and wrapped around her throat. Unable to breathe, Leona tried unsuccessfully to discreetly wiggle her fingers free. Glass-shard tingles raced from her oxygen-deprived head to her throbbing feet.

Her feet? Oh no!

She'd been so concerned about David and Maxine and Roy and Saul she hadn't noticed until this very minute that her toes were screaming in protest. From the corner of her eye, she could see Saul. Her smug ex-lawyer seemed as comfortable in his shiny shoes as he was with Ruthie's arm looped through his. Leona scooted closer to Roy, which only made her breathing more difficult.

The room began to spin. Leona was on the verge of asking Roy to take her home when Kendra said, "To keep the soles of your dance shoes in pristine condition, they must never be worn outside the studio."

Leona glanced at her shoes again. Gravel dents pocked the satin on the toe box. No telling how much damage picking her way across the parking lot had done to her soles. She'd been so swept up by Roy's charms, she'd failed to use her head. She hated making mistakes, especially stupid ones.

"We're going to start with the box step." Kendra clapped her hands twice to signal she was now getting down to business. "Gentlemen, take your partner's hand and put her on your right side."

Roy quickly complied, placing himself squarely between Leona and Saul. Too late to leave now. "Breathe through your nose, LeLe."

She managed a pained nod.

"Now, my partner and I are going to turn our backs on y'all." Kendra waved to a lanky fellow lurking in the shadows and the young man did a light-foot sprint to her side.

"That's Angus," Leona whispered to Roy.

"The boy from the diner?" Roy asked.

Leona clasped her tightening chest. "Can this night get any stranger?"

"Breathe, LeLe," Roy urged again.

Once everyone had scurried into position, Kendra laid the

microphone on an empty chair, took Angus by the hand, and began shouting her instructions. "Feet together." Kendra's heels came together and Leona did her best to force her feet to comply. "Step forward with the left foot. Slide to the right. When your feet come together, your weight must shift to your left foot." She and Angus slid effortlessly across the floor. No one moved. "And then repeat," Kendra said, without turning around to count the casualties. She and Angus slid in unison again, their movements creating the outline of a perfect box on the floor.

Roy looked at Leona. "Ready to give 'er a go, LeLe?"

She nodded. The step forward went well enough, but during the slide, Roy's big red and black shoes caught her heel. She stumbled, crashing into Roy. They ended up in a tangled mess that nearly put them on their butts. Leona gave the room a quick survey. Sadly, she and Roy were the only casualties. Everyone else had mastered the simple step beautifully…including Saul and Ruthie.

Kendra and Angus carried on as if everyone was a natural. "Now, let's go backwards," Kendra said. "Right foot back. Slide to the left. Feet together."

"Now let's take our dance position." Kendra and her partner turned and faced each other. "Positions, everyone." She waited until everyone had copied their stance.

Leona and Roy awkwardly turned and faced each other. For the first time, Leona realized the top of her head didn't clear Roy's shoulder...even in two-inch heels.

Kendra held her right hand high. "The man's left hand takes the lady's right." Angus's hand met Kendra's mid-air. "To complete the hold, the man's right hand comes around, slides beneath the woman's left arm, and comes to rest on the woman's left shoulder blade like so." Kendra waited until Angus held her properly then she turned her head and smiled out at her class as if they were her children. "Positions, everyone."

Roy and Leona raised their hands and lowered them like they were confused traffic cops. After several unsuccessful attempts and near-misses, they finally managed to connect. Now that they were holding hands, Leona put her hand on Roy's shoulder. Roy's other hand was a grappling hook somewhere between her waist and bra line. They were coupled, but their stance fell woefully short of mimicking the perfect scene before them.

Roy, however, was convinced they'd finally pulled it off. "Let's go, LeLe." He yanked her close. Her face smushed against the chest hairs protruding from the top buttons he'd left undone.

"Roy!" Leona sputtered, tossing her head back for a snatch

of air.

"Not so tight, Roy." Kendra said, coming to Leona's rescue.

"Oh." His arms dropped. "Sorry, LeLe."

Leona backed up, her nose still twitching from the hairy irritation. From the corner of her eye, she could see that Saul and Ruthie had matched up perfectly. Leona lifted her chin and turned her attention squarely back on Roy. "Don't worry, Roy. It's a lot harder than it looks on *Dancing with the Stars*."

"What?" he asked, obviously behind on American T.V.

"Never mind." Leona stepped forward and guided his right hand to her left shoulder blade.

"The key is to mirror your partner." Kendra and Angus proceeded to demonstrate the ease by which a simple box step could be used to create all sorts of dances.

Angus stepped forward. Kendra stepped back. Stepping and sliding, the well-matched pair glided across the floor. "What makes this simple step a waltz is the lowering and rising of the dancers' bodies," Kendra shouted as she and Angus waltzed around like they were auditioning for a dance show. Once they were finished showing off, they whirled to a stop and Kendra said, "Okay, y'all. See how easy it is? Let me see you give it a try."

Leona felt every muscle in her body tense.

Roy leaned forward and said, "Relax, LeLe. We've got this."

But they didn't. They stopped and started and stopped and started. Dancing was never this hard with J.D. and they'd never had a single lesson. Maybe it was her partner? No. She refused to let her mind go there. "Ouch."

"Sorry, LeLe," Roy apologized for the tenth time. "Guess J.D. wasn't the only one with two left feet."

She'd always admired those people who'd never danced before who were willing to make a fool of themselves and try. Not that she wanted to be anyone's fool. In fact, that was the last thing she ever wanted to be. But if she was to ever be free of her need to please everyone, dancing seemed like a good first step.

Maybe she should have tried knitting.

While everyone else progressed on to the next step, Kendra assigned Angus to help her and Roy. Over and over, Angus patiently walked them through the steps until finally, Leona had to ask for a break. "I need to catch my breath," she told Roy then darted for the restroom.

She locked the door to the single commode and ripped off her shoe. An ugly blister bulged from the first joint of her little toe. She dug through her purse searching for the miniature first aid kit she kept on hand. It took a few minutes to wiggle out of her pantyhose. She flipped the toilet seat lid and plopped down. After she applied the Band- Aid, she shimmied into her pantyhose. Cramming her swollen foot into the ill-fitting shoe felt like she was one of Cinderella's ugly stepsisters.

What was she trying to prove? She wasn't twenty-one and carefree. She was a fifty-two-year-old widow who'd been happily married for nearly thirty years. What made her think a few turns around the dance floor would make her feel alive again?

She closed her purse and went to the sink to wash her hands. She stared into the mirror. Tears threatened to ruin the eyeliner Roxie insisted she wear.

Roy joked like J.D.

Roy was tall like J.D.

Roy even sort of kissed like J.D., assertive and expectant.

But Roy McGee was not J.D. She missed her husband.

A knock at the door jarred the ugly truth loose. J.D. was gone and hiding in a gas station bathroom wasn't going to bring him back.

"Just a minute." Leona ripped a wad of tissue from the roll and dabbed at the streaks beneath her eyes. She'd paid good money for these lessons and she wasn't going to quit until she'd given learning to dance her best shot. She threw the tissue in the trash and unlocked the door.

When she returned to the lobby, the music in the ballroom had been turned off. Couples had migrated to the lobby where they were pulling water bottles and Gatorade from their backpacks, along with candy bars and apples. Laughter filled the space that used to double as a small grocery store. Roy stood behind the old check-out counter telling fascinating tales of lion attacks, elephants trampling village gardens, and men beating crocs away so he could baptize people in the muddy rivers.

Roy was loud, funny, and irresistible. It was almost as if J.D. had been reincarnated.

Saul handed her a bottle of water. "He's something, isn't he?"

"Yes." Exactly *what* she didn't know, but definitely something. She unscrewed her drink lid and took a long, deep gulp. She wiped the dribble on her chin, expecting Saul to take the hint that she was in no mood to talk to him and move on. But he stood there. Saying nothing. Waiting patiently on her to finish. She swallowed and said, "Enjoying the class?"

"I am," Saul admitted, enthusiastically. "Ruthie's quite light on her feet."

"Must run in the Crouch DNA. Angus is pretty impressive as well."

"That kid is full of surprises, isn't he?"

Leona couldn't help but turn. She was pleased to see the same thaw toward Angus in Saul's expression that she'd heard in his voice. "I wonder where the boy learned to dance?"

"Ruthie's been teaching him." Saul sipped his water. "They push the tables back after they close the diner. Then they pop a few quarters into the jukebox and dance until Ruthie's feet give out."

She'd noticed the lights on in the diner a few nights ago when she'd stayed late at the paper, but it never occurred to her to peek in the windows. "Ruthie will miss him when he goes off to school."

"Not sure he's going."

"What do you mean?"

"Angus didn't get his scholarship."

A shocked gasp escaped Leona's throat. "I didn't know." Before she could tell Saul she wasn't about to let Angus or his talents waste away in Mt. Hope, Kendra called the class back to order.

"This time," Kendra said as she danced to the music system, "I want each of you to choose a new partner." The music cued up and excitement throbbed through the class.

Ruthie looped her arm through Roy's. "I'll take on this tall drink of water." She pulled Roy to the ballroom.

Everyone paired up in a flurry, leaving Leona and Saul alone in the deserted lobby. Music drifted in from the ballroom, but the smooth notes did not fill the uncomfortable silence.

"I believe I owe you a dance." Saul offered his hand.

"What makes you think that?"

"I was rude when you invited me to dance at your son's wedding reception."

She stared at his open palm. "Well, if we're making amends, I owe *you* an apology."

"For?"

"The things I said," she admitted.

"Before or after you fired me."

"Both." She threw her empty water bottle in the trash. "I know you're far too honorable to bilk a widow."

He lowered his hand. "The thought of paying my fee isn't what made you mad." Why did this man have to make everything so difficult?

"You were right." There she said it, but the admission stuck in her throat like day-old grits. "I need to let my children work out their own lives." She blinked back tears.

"Easier said than done." An unfamiliar tone, one she could only interpret as kindness, had softened his voice.

She nodded, glancing furtively through the open doors leading to the ballroom. Roy was doing just fine with Ruthie as his partner. They were gliding about the polished floors and laughing like dancing was every bit as easy as the professionals made it seem.

Maybe she was the problem. The thought struck such a hard blow, she felt her knees give.

Saul offered his left hand. "Dance with me."

Her gaze drifted back to Roy. "Obviously, I'm not very good."

"I am."

Her gaze cut back to the self-assured man before her. "And humble."

His eyes locked hers with an intensity she couldn't have broken if she wanted to. "Humility is overrated." His fingers motioned her forward.

She put her hand in his. The warm tingly feeling she'd experienced with Roy did not race up her arm. Saul's calloused squeeze instantly dispersed her disappointment. His touch, a strong, steady comfort, enveloped her. She felt equally compelled to return the comfort.

In an instant, he had her in his arms. "Lean into me and let me help guide you."

Eye to eye, an energy she could not resist held her

captive. Saul stepped forward with his left foot. Her right foot instinctively stepped backward. "That's the ticket," he said firmly. "Now, slide. And step."

"Do you smell bananas?" tumbled from her quivering lips after they completed their first box step without a single mishap.

A true, full-on pleased smile lifted Saul's mustache and set off a sparkle in his sky blue eyes. "Use the peels to oil my shoes."

"Really?"

"Old military trick." He applied pressure to her shoulder and moved her snugly against his solid chest. Her chin hovered just above his shoulder. He placed his cheek against hers and whispered, "Dance, Leona."

With her name warm against her neck, and the brush of his mustache on her face, she relaxed in his arms. Before she knew what happened, she and Saul were whirling around the lobby in a cloud of navy chiffon.

CHAPTER TEN

Leona's van coughed to a stop in the parking slot between the Koffee Kup and the Mt. Hope Messenger. With last night's blister throbbing, she was exceptionally grateful Ruthie had granted her parking privileges so close to the diner and work. A familiar sports coat flashed into Leona's peripheral view. She looked to find Angus knocking on her window.

Seeing her dead husband's clothes brought to life twisted the feelings she'd spent the night sorting into a painful knot. Angus needed J.D.'s suits. She couldn't let every sighting of the ratty sports coat send her into a tailspin. What if her pain didn't have a thing to do with J.D.'s castoff wardrobe? Roxie was wrong when she said the turmoil in Leona's belly stemmed from her unrelenting guilt for being alive. The pain stemmed from falling in love with the wrong man.

Love? Where had that come from? Women her age didn't *fall* in love after one dance class. She was just missing J.D., that's all.

"Morning, Miss Leona," Angus waved, obviously not the least bit worn out from his night of dance instructing. "I've got the coffee on whenever you're ready to come in."

She nodded then snatched her keys from the ignition. She limped into the diner as gracefully as the blister on her foot would allow. Her eyes shot past Angus waiting at the door with a welcoming smile and a menu.

Saul's booth was empty. She looked at her watch. Six-thirty-two. Where was he? Had last night interrupted his sleep as it had hers? She lowered her arm. What was it to her how Saul Levy interpreted their dance? They'd both danced with several different people after that. With any luck, he'd probably already forgotten about all the times she stepped on his feet.

"Booth or table, Miss Leona?" Angus asked.

"Uh, a table by the window please, Angus. Oh, and I'm waiting on David so I'll need a couple of coffees and two ice waters when you get a minute." She limped toward an empty table.

"You raised more on the dance floor last night than that blister you're nursing, Miss Leona."

Heat flushing her cheeks, she positioned herself so she could watch the door and Saul's booth at the same time. "Just bring the coffee, would you please, Angus?"

Angus scowled, obviously confused by her refusal to talk about what he perceived to be a wonderful evening. He wasn't the only one. Roy sulked the entire drive back to her house because she'd been so quiet.

"Sure thing, Miss Leona." He shot to the drink station, returned with full hands, and approached the topic from a different direction. "You and Mister Saul sure looked like you were havin' fun at the dance."

"I enjoyed the class," she admitted, hoping he'd leave it at that.

"No offense, but I don't think you and Mister Roy are a good match."

Apparently, Angus wasn't going to leave what happened last night alone. Why should he? It was a fairy tale moment he'd probably only seen in the movies. The sound of everyone clapping when she and Saul ended their first dance still roared in her ears. The feel of his body pressed against hers still flowed through her veins.

But she didn't want to discuss the differences between Roy and Saul any more than she wanted to be the topic of local gossip, so she changed the subject. "I didn't know you were such a good dancer, Angus. You are so light on your feet."

"I have my MeMaw to thank for that." He slid the menu in front of her. "She's determined to teach me the good graces before I head off to school." He leaned in, glanced over his shoulder, then whispered, "I didn't have the heart to tell her college kids don't waltz."

"So you got the scholarship worked out?"

"Yes, ma'am." He set a glass of ice water on her table. "I think anyway. I'm a little confused."

"About what?"

"Last week I got this letter from the dean sayin' I didn't get the scholarship." He pulled a folded piece of paper from one of J.D.'s jacket pockets. "Then yesterday I got this certified letter from the very same man sayin' I got more than a scholarship." He handed her that letter, too. "I got my whole way paid. Room, board, tuition, books, and a five-hundred-dollar-a-month spending allowance. What do you think happened, Miss Leona?"

Leona read *anonymous contributor* and her heart sank. "I don't know." She'd only learned about the plight of Angus's lost scholarship last night. One of the reasons she'd asked David to meet her this morning was so that he could help her arrange something similar by funneling her money through the church. Who had taken such good care of Angus Freestone while she dreamed of dancing? She folded his mail and handed the letters back. "An unexpected blessing, for sure."

"Manna from heaven, MeMaw says." His grin was as big as the lunch-special dinner plates as he stuffed the papers inside his suit pocket. He slid her coffee in front of her. "I'll pour Mister David's coffee when he comes. Anything else I can get while you wait?"

The bell above the diner door jangled.

"Well, speak of the devil," Angus announced. "Gotcha a table over here, Mister David."

David strode across the diner. "Hey, Momma." He kissed her cheek then turned to their waiter. "Angus, you owe me a game of basketball."

"Name the time and place." Angus slapped down another menu. "Coffee?"

"Only if you made it," David teased.

"Hint of salt. Just the way you like it," Angus said. "You heard my good news, Mister David?"

"Someone has gifted Angus a full ride to Abilene Christian," Leona announced, keeping a close eye on David's reaction.

David's surprised look as he clapped Angus on the back told Leona her son hadn't used his share of the inheritance to fund Angus's education. "Four years from now you'll be buyin' my breakfast."

Once Angus left with their orders and a promise to return with another round of coffee, Leona poked a little deeper. "You changed that boy's life."

"He changed mine, Momma." David took a sip, eyeing her carefully over the rim. "Someone else looks changed this morning. Guess I was wrong about the dancing. You obviously had fun."

"I did."

"Roxie told me Roy took you."

"Hell's bells, David." Leona jammed a fist on either side of her waist and shook her head exactly the way her best friend did. "You know you can't believe everything that redhead says." They both chuckled at her overdone impersonation.

"I like Roy." David reached for her hand. "He's ..."

"A lot like your father?" Saying the words out loud had a strange and sobering effect on her, an effect David picked up immediately, judging from the quirk in his brow.

"Amazing was the word I was looking for."

She peeled the foil back on one of those tiny creamer cups and poured the contents into her coffee. "He's asked me to go to Africa with him."

David's face brightened. "You said yes, right?"

"I haven't said anything … yet."

"Why not?"

"Because someone I know is going to have my first grandchild."

"Glad to know you're excited."

"Of course I am, David. But I can't leave knowing Amy and this baby could have a rough time of it."

"Momma, there'll always be a reason for you to stay," David said. "Go to Africa if that'll make you happy. We want you to be happy."

"I *am* happy."

"You're going through the motions, but the spark…it went out when Dad died and I hadn't seen it return until Roy came to town."

"David, I think you're reading far more into Roy's return than—"

"Go see the world, Momma. You've always wanted to. You can afford to fly home if we need you."

If they need me? Saul was right. She was a meddling old fool. "You don't want me—"

"Momma, who tried to talk you out of moving out of the parsonage? Me." His genuine love for her cut her worries off at the knees. "But only a selfish brat would insist on having his mother hold his hand forever." He raised his palm. "Hear me out."

"You came back to Mt. Hope for me."

"But I stayed for me and you know that, Momma." David's face softened. "Tomorrow, Amy and I are telling the congregation about the baby. The moment the service is over, you know Nola Gay and Etta May will launch the prayer chain. The Lord's got us covered."

"Why tomorrow?"

"It's Sunday, remember?"

"Of course."

David's face puzzled. "Are you worried about something else?"

"I think Maddie might like to be here when you make it official," she covered.

"Probably." He shrugged. "But she's busy, Momma."

"Your sister has been in on this plan of yours and Amy's from the start. I think she'll want to see it to a successful conclusion."

"Something tells me this is about more than letting Maddie play the role of proud aunt. It's even more than getting Maddie back in church, right?"

"If you wait a week, that will give me time to work out flying Maddie home and possibly planning a little celebration or baby shower or something. Nothing big. Just a few of your closest friends."

He studied her for a second. "You plan to kill two birds with one stone, don't you?"

"I don't know what you're talking about."

"Admit it. You don't want Parker to leave without Maddie giving their relationship one last shot."

"Well, sue me."

"Momma, my sister and I appreciate everything you've ever done for us. Really, we do. But we don't want you to blow your chance at happiness because you were busy trying to arrange ours."

Angus delivered steaming plates of bacon and eggs with sides of biscuits, gravy, and grits.

"Well, there is one more little matter I've debated whether or not to tell you about," Leona said between bites.

"You *are* eloping with Roy."

"No." The adamancy in her voice surprised her. "This isn't about me. It's about Maxine and Howard."

The playfulness on David's face disappeared. "What now?"

She leaned across the table and whispered, "Maxine and Howard could divorce."

David dropped his fork. "What?"

"She believes Howard is having an affair. If that's the case, it will change the makeup of the board."

"And a change on the board could possibly change my current level of support?"

"You've worked hard to win that group of people over. With the board you have now, you know what to expect. But bring on someone new, who knows?"

"A bigger question is what can I do to help them?" David raked his hair. "I don't have enough years of a marriage experience behind me to offer them credible counseling."

"If it's not overstepping, I have an idea."

"Momma, you've got experience I don't have."

Pleased she wasn't completely washed-up, Leona continued, "When I mentioned to Amy that I wanted to help her convert your old room into a nursery, she said to wait until after you made the announcement to the church." She framed her next words carefully. "Why don't I invite Maxine to help us paint?"

David shook his head. "Momma, it's bad enough that Maxine is always telling me how to run the church. I don't want her telling my wife how beige to make our child's room."

Leona held up her palm. "Maxine and I used to paint together all the time. We redid all of the children's classrooms in the church. We've had great conversations over a paint tray. Let me see if working together again will open the door she slammed so long ago. After all, she came to me. Let me try talking to her. See if I can't get to the bottom of this."

David let out a long, resigned sigh. "Do you think it's true, Momma?"

Maxine's distraught face flashed in Leona's mind. "I think marriage is hard. People don't mean to hurt each other, but sometimes things happen. Pain can push people apart. When we're hurting, we're all capable of behaving in ways we never thought possible."

"I wish Colton hadn't died."

"Me, too."

"Morning, Leona." The same male voice that had encouraged her last night encouraged her now.

Leona's head snapped up. Saul stood beside their table, a newspaper in his hand. The headline she'd written introducing the new dance studio to the community was on the front page. What if he wanted to talk about their dance? What if he brought up David's baby? She'd told him that in confidence when she thought her secrets were protected by attorney-client privilege. But she couldn't expect an intoxicating spin around the dance floor to keep his lips sealed. Could she?

"Nice write-up about Kendra's studio," Saul said, snapping Leona from her frantic wonderings. "She'll appreciate the publicity, I'm sure." He nodded to David. "Your mother's a talented woman."

Oh no! Leona shifted in her seat, bracing for ... she wasn't sure.

"Thanks," David's tone was less than cordial.

From the hardening of Saul's jaw, he'd gotten the message. "I'll leave you to your eggs. Nice seeing you ... both." He executed a sharp pivot and strode toward his usual booth where Angus was already setting him up with coffee.

Leona didn't realize she'd quit breathing until David poked her. "Momma?"

Saul had not betrayed her in any way, shape, or form. "Yes."

"I'm thanking God."

"Why?"

"It could have been that gold-digging ambulance chaser that asked you to go to Africa."

"He's not a gold digger," slipped softly from her lips but her eyes remained glued on the man having coffee alone.

"I'm glad you fired him."

CHAPTER ELEVEN

Looking forward to a Sunday afternoon of painting, Leona tossed her red heels in the closet and peeled off her dress. She wanted her guest bedroom to feel like home when Maddie came next weekend. It hadn't taken much to convince her daughter to juggle her hospital schedule. Maddie's quick agreement seemed strange, especially since she'd been too busy to come to Mt. Hope since David and Amy's wedding. Leona had a sneaky suspicion David may have put a bug in his sister's ear about the possibility of their mother running off to Africa.

If she'd have known that's all it would take to bring Maddie back to Mt. Hope, she would have found someone to threaten to run off with a year ago.

She hadn't decided one way or the other on Roy or his

offer to see the world, but she had to admit, it was nice having a man sitting beside her on the pew. The charming missionary had so many wonderful qualities. His commitment to the Lord, along with his desire to make a difference in the world, was so like J.D. But something deep inside of her froze whenever Roy reached for her hand. Since the dance lesson date, he seemed to be reaching for her with increased regularity. Maybe it was all just too fast. Maybe Roy wasn't the right man for her second chance. Maybe God had only planned one chance at love for her and she'd used that one up.

Leona yanked her favorite paint-splattered shirt over her head, catching a glimpse of herself in the mirror. The colors on the shirt were from her old life, her life as the pastor's wife in the parsonage. Determined to rid her new house of the same beige, she ripped the shirt off and tossed it in the trash.

She dug through the stack of tees in her dresser drawer. She chose a pale blue one, pulling the soft, worn fabric over her head and running her palm over the blank canvas. Every new splatter would be the color of her choosing and on walls she owned.

On her way to the garage for supplies, she popped her Gaither CD in the new stereo system she'd bought. Not exactly ballroom tempo, but a tempo she and J.D. loved. She held her right hand high, closed her eyes. Right foot back.

Step. Slide. She imagined herself waltzing around the dance floor, gliding and swaying in the arms of Saul...what? Her eyes popped open. Goosebumps pimpled her flesh. Her breath came out in short puffs, her heart thumped her chest.

She'd seen Saul out of the corner of her eye after church. Not accidentally. She'd looked for him. She wanted to thank him for keeping his knowledge of David's baby to himself, and for not mentioning their dance, and for ... it didn't really matter because as she was making her way down the aisle, Roy whisked her over to talk to Maxine and Howard. The pair was so miserably uncomfortable and Roy was so completely oblivious, Leona didn't have the heart to excuse herself from the situation. By the time Roy was finished shoring up his donor base, Saul was gone.

The military attorney was all wrong for her. David was right. Roy and his mission-minded ways fit her far better. Think of Roy, Leona told herself as she gathered supplies in the garage.

Arms loaded, she sighed at the dog. "Let's do this, Tater." The cocker trotted down the hall and dropped outside the door to the guest room.

Thirty minutes later, she'd pushed Saul from her mind and shoved the furniture to the center of the room. She draped the exposed hardwoods in plastic, took a flathead screwdriver to the lid on the paint can, and pried it open. She filled a new paint tray and dipped the roller in the dreamy shade of designer gray. Maxine had vehemently refused to let her use anything other than beige in the parsonage. She claimed keeping the parsonage neutral made the house more appealing. For whom? Leona had always wanted to ask. The next pastor?

Leona cranked her Gaither CD as loud as it would go then began to roll paint. With each stroke, the beige she'd lived with so long disappeared.

When she had one wall coated and cut in, she stepped back to admire her work. She was enjoying being able to paint her house any color, anytime she liked. No longer did she have to worry what anyone thought.

Empowered by the freedom, she perched the roller on the edge of the tray and checked her cell phone. Before she could change her mind, she tapped out a text.

Saul. Your discretion in regards to David and Amy's baby was much appreciated. Thanks. Leona

Her children told her she didn't have to sign her texts, but this wasn't just any text. This was a formal-slash-casual expression of gratitude.

Finger hovering over SEND, she checked her wording. Nothing wrong with sending a simple thank you. In all her years of ministry, she'd never received a single gift that she hadn't immediately acknowledged with a written thank you. Gratitude had always been one of her more endearing traits. Not that she wanted to endear herself in any way, shape or form to Saul Levy. But the man deserved credit where credit was due. Keeping her message digital instead of handwritten kept her sentiments from seeming too personal. If Saul Levy was as smart as he thought he was, he could read between the lines and know how much she appreciated his decision to keep their dance to himself as well.

Before she could change her mind, she pushed SEND. Hands trembling, her breath caught in her throat. She stared at the blank screen, waiting for a response. Nothing.

Well, she'd done the right thing. Now that her conscience was clear, maybe she could concentrate on the bigger decision looming before her...what to do about Roy McGee?

"Leona!" her mother's voice called from the living room. "You here?"

Tater sprang into action, barking and snarling.

"In the back." Leona pocketed her phone and stepped into the hall.

"Call off this killer, Leona." Bertie clung to Cotton's arm.

"Tater! Leave it." The dog obediently dropped at Leona's feet. "Y'all come on back. I'm painting the guest room before

Maddie comes home."

Bertie kept a wary eye on the dog as she made her way down the hall.

"Looks like you're settling in," Cotton said as he trailed Leona's mother. "I believe you can do anything you set your mind to, Leona."

"No wonder Mother loves you," she winked at the snowy-headed man who'd made her husband a very rich man. If she could forgive Cotton for his part in the conspiracy, why was she having such a hard time letting J.D. or Saul off the hook? "Watch your step." She led them into the room.

Bertie and Cotton maneuvered around the dresser blocking the door and stood on the plastic.

"What do you think?" Leona asked, hands on hips and a prideful smile on her face.

"I think this place is so small if you get bit by a mosquito you won't have room to swell." Her mother's standard assessment of Leona's choices was no surprise. "Why don't you spend some of your money and build a house on one of the lake lots close to me and Cotton? There are still several prime spots for sale right on the water. Your lawyer bought one. He lives on one of the private coves now, you know?

"No, I didn't." Leona tried to picture Saul motoring about on a fishing boat, sipping sweet tea in the clubhouse, or leisurely strolling the banks at sunset. "And I don't have a lawyer."

"That Levy fellow doesn't represent you?" Bertie asked.

"I fired him."

"Oh." Mother hated being the last to know things.

"Well, I fired him and then I apologized and … truth is … I'm not sure where we stand at the moment." While many areas in Leona's relationship with her mother had improved since she'd eloped with Cotton, feeling the need to justify her every decision wasn't one of them.

"Who's handling your affairs?" Bertie asked.

"I am."

She braced for a lecture on her lack of experience managing such large sums. Instead, her mother said, "You're a very capable and smart woman, Leona. You'll do fine."

"Really?"

"Really," Bertie said.

Encouraged by such rare praise, Leona waved her hand toward the freshly painted walls. "So, what do you think of the color?"

"It's lovely."

"Who are you, and what have you done with my mother?" Leona asked.

"People can change, Leona." Her mother had changed since she married Cotton and if this little snippet of praise was any indication, she'd changed for the better.

"I want Maddie to feel at home."

"If you want her to stay, you should have left the beige." Bertie shrugged at Leona's pointed glare. "A zebra can't change its stripes overnight."

"Home with a new spin, then." Talking to her mother was like strolling a field of hidden land mines.

"David told me the news."

Leona reached over and put the lid on the paint can. "I'm trying not to worry."

"Since when?"

"Since I decided I'd never liked beige and would never paint anything that bland color again."

"There is cause for concern, though, isn't there?"

The real reason for her mother's visit suddenly became clear. "Yes."

"What are you doing to ensure my great grandchild arrives safely?"

"I tried to have Saul convince the hospital board to hire a maternal-fetal specialist, but he didn't think my idea was viable."

"You fired him?"

"You know, Mother. I don't think I ever fully understood how difficult it was for you to sit back and watch me make decisions you didn't agree with until now. As much as I hate to admit it, Saul was right. Amy's prenatal health care is David and Amy's decision."

Bertie patted the back of her hair, her default tick when she knew she'd pushed too far. "I think Great Granny sounds terribly old, don't you?"

"I dare anyone to call *you* Granny."

Bertie's gaze looked the room over. "You know, if you're not going to invest your millions in an expensive lake property, you can afford to hire your redecorating done, right?"

Relieved her mother had chosen to abandon her attempts to interfere in David's life, Leona smiled. "Painting gives me a chance to think about things."

"Things like whether or not you're going to Africa?" Bertie asked.

"Now, Bertie," Cotton put his hand on her mother's shoulder. "We agreed we weren't going to pry."

"It's not prying when it comes to *my* child, dear," Bertie replied, sweetly putting her new husband in his place.

"How did you find out about—" Leona stopped. "Let me guess. The Storys."

"Nola Gay and Etta May heard Roy telling Maxine and Howard all about his plans to show you the world." Bertie took her hand. "Frankly, I'm thrilled for you, Leona."

"Mother, I can't go."

"Why not?"

"David and Amy's baby for starters."

"Didn't you just say you delivered and raised two perfectly wonderful children without me hovering over you?"

"That was different."

"Leona, I don't think your reluctance has a thing to do with the pending arrival of your grandchild." Bertie took her hands. "But it has everything to do with your reluctance to love again."

"J.D. used up all my love."

"My dear, sweet girl, you've got more love in you than ten of me." Bertie paused, obviously weighing her words carefully. "Life is short. If you get a second chance to dance, then dance with everything that is in you." Bertie looped her arm through Cotton's. "That's why this man and I are setting off for a Mediterranean cruise tomorrow. We didn't know about David's little announcement and I'm afraid it's too late to change our plans."

"Cruising?"

"Dancing our way from Catalonia to Greece."

She'd always thought it would be romantic to dance upon the top deck of a beautiful ship, but deep water and shallow pockets had always kept her from thinking such a dream would ever come true. "Sounds divine."

"It's not too late to come with us."

"It is for me, Mother."

"I booked an extra passage in hopes you'd change your mind."

"You know how I am about water, Mother." Leona's phone dinged. She froze. Wide-eyed. Too afraid to peek at the possibility Saul had responded after all.

Bertie pointed at Leona's pocket. "Are you going to answer that?"

"It can wait."

"What if it's one of the kids?"

"You're right." Leona slowly pulled her phone from her pocket. One quick glance and she could tell the message *was* from Saul. Wait. She glanced again, her brow furrowing as she read. His response was not the response she'd expected. She looked up, her hands trembling. "I need a moment."

Cotton was the first to catch the quandary on her face. "Bertie, if we're going to take the boat out to catch the sunset, we need to get a move on."

Bertie pointed at Leona's phone. "Tell him you'll meet him." A sly smile crossed her mother's lips.

"You don't know who it is."

"Doesn't matter. He makes your eyes light up." Bertie took

Cotton's arm. "Oh, and you might want to change out of those paint clothes before you go, Leona."

"He's just a friend, Mother."

Bertie smiled at Cotton. "Friends make the best husbands."

Leona waited until Cotton had backed her mother's new car from the drive. She read the text slowly. Word for word. Again. And again.

Would you like to practice the dance steps we learned together?

Together? Saul remembered their dance. Had it meant as much to him as it had to her?

Leona glanced at the paint drying in the tray. She poked a hole into the paint's thin crust with the screwdriver. Wet, vibrant color poured through the opening. Life beneath the surface.

Yes. When? She responded.

Will pick you up in an hour.

Heart thumping she tapped out *Ok*.

Bring your dance shoes. And a sweater.

CHAPTER TWELVE

While her heart was soaring, her feet were cement blocks she could barely drag to the door. What if dancing with Saul Levy was a big mistake? She hated making mistakes.

"It's such a beautiful afternoon, do you mind if I put the top down on the car?" Saul asked as he led her to the passenger door of his Lexus.

He'd arrived thirty minutes early, which didn't surprise her. That he looked like a man more comfortable on the golf course than the courtroom had taken her breath. He'd traded his suit for an untucked Burberry oxford the same sky blue color of his eyes. White cotton twill shorts exposed his tan, muscular legs. But it was the boat shoes without socks that made her grateful she'd chosen capris and strappy sandals instead of the skirt and hose she'd first considered.

"Glad you remembered your sweater." He opened the passenger door. "The evening breeze off the lake is often chilly."

"The lake?" The terrifying sensation of the car careening over a bridge and plunging into water swept through her. Who was left to save her?

Saul slid into the driver's seat. "My dock mimics the feel of the boards at Kendra's studio."

She'd never pictured Saul Levy as an outdoor man, let alone someone who appreciated the feel of swaying boards beneath his dance shoes. Throat closing, she gasped, "We're dancing *on* the water?"

Alerted by the panic in her voice, he cut her a sideways glance. "I've got a screened in patio if you're worried about the mosquitos."

Unwilling to let him see another of her faults, she let out a slow breath, "Mother mentioned you'd moved to the lake."

"Bertie and Cotton regularly troll my cove in that monster fishing rig of theirs."

"It's bigger than my house, but they love it." She'd only been to Bertie and Cotton's home on the lake one time because of their attempt to coax her aboard the *Good Investment*, as they'd christened the sleek bass boat. And they'd made that trip at night so she didn't have to see the water, but she knew it was there.

Truth be known, her decision to buy a small house in town rather than near her mother had been influenced as much by her desire to stay away from deep water as it was to keep her fortune a secret. Since J.D. died, she'd felt like she was drowning. She'd finally floated to the surface enough to move into her own house and learn to dance. Conquering her fear of water could wait.

Saul pushed a button on the dash and the car purred to life. "Ready?"

She worked to get a handle on the panic as they sped past the city limits. After all, she was fairly confident Saul wasn't planning to throw her in the lake. The man simply wanted some privacy to work on their dance steps.

Enveloped in the plush, soft leather of his Lexus, the thought hit her. Was this a date? When Roy took her to dance lessons, his overt advances had made it clear he considered their time together a date. She and Saul had never been on an official date. Technically, he'd called this a practice session.

Was she splitting hairs? Her time in front of the mirror and pacing the living room window had all the markings of a woman anticipating the arrival of her date. If she'd really thought through Saul's offer before she accepted, she probably would've passed. But she hadn't. And now the prospect of being alone with Saul Levy was nearly as unsettling as being near the water.

To keep her mind from diving in murky pools, Leona began to concentrate on the countryside. Scrub cedar and twisted mesquites dotted the flat landscape stretching for miles in every direction. When she and J.D. first arrived in West Texas she'd thought of the place as God-forsaken. After living here this long, she now saw freedom and possibilities.

As if Saul had sensed her need to collect herself, he'd remained quiet for the next ten minutes. Wind whipping her hair, Leona found her date's silence surprisingly comforting and completely different from Roy's constant reminiscing. But then, she and Saul had no history. Their relationship was a blank slate. Completely devoid of joint memories—unless she counted their mutual involvement in her husband's financial affairs or the night Saul carried her to bed after she ingested pot brownies. And those limited encounters had been so bumpy and humiliating, she was grateful he wasn't inclined to bring them up.

The increase of trees on the barren landscape meant they were nearing the water. She held tight to the armrest as they sped over the dam, keeping her eyes on the road rather than the height of the lake level from an abnormally wet spring.

She didn't breathe again until they'd cleared lake.

Saul slowed and wheeled his Lexus through an arched wrought-iron entry gate. Expansive houses were nestled among the trees that hugged the shore.

"No wonder Mother loves it out here." Leona inhaled deeply, the faint scent of water dampening the tang of cattle and wild sage in her nostrils. She'd never ridden with the wind in her face and if it weren't for this nagging sense of plunging into a watery grave, the exhilaration pumping through her veins would have been completely glorious. "I didn't know such beauty existed in West Texas."

"Oil paid for most of these houses."

"It's not just the houses. The whole setting seems out of place."

"Water makes all the difference."

"Hmmm," she agreed, panic pushing back the water's proximity. She forced her mind to dwell on the enterprise that had financed Saul's ability to live in this upscale neighborhood. "Which one is yours?"

"I'm on a little cove at the end of the road."

A quarter of a mile later, the pavement ended. Saul eased his car onto a narrow dirt lane. A canopy of red oaks and cypress trees towered overhead. To her right, Leona noticed an old rock chimney surrounded by the ruins of what must have been an early settler's cabin. A few gravestones protruded from the weeds.

"My wife's family was one of the first to settle in the territory." Saul pointed toward the chimney. "That's all that's left of the original homestead."

"What was your wife's name?"

"Claire." He let the car idle down the lane. While the fact that he'd inherited this place from a woman she'd never asked about rolled around in her head, Saul let the Lexus roll to a stop beside a small stone building. "Here we are."

Leona's gaze took in the cottage set on a rise that overlooked the lake. A thicket of mesquite and scrub brush cocooned the single-story structure on three sides. Slabs of Hill Country limestone had been meticulously puzzled-pieced together over the outside of the house from foundation to roof peak. Rough cedar casings framed a bank of sparkling floor-to-ceiling windows and thick cedar beams supported the stunning wrap-around porch. Cozy bentwood chairs with colorful cushions were grouped around a handcrafted wooden coffee table perfect for propping one's feet while sipping a delicious cup of coffee. Someone had obviously invested a massive amount of time and attention into making this secluded spot a magical retreat from the world.

"You live here?" she asked, trying to picture such an

uptight person surviving in such an untamed habitat.

"Moved in a couple of months ago." He opened his door. "Took me three years to evict all the furry varmints and make it livable." He came around and opened her door. "Want the nickel look-see or the dollar tour?"

"I'm feeling generous." She gathered her purse, shoes, and sweater. She took his hand, fully aware that if he'd done all this work, he'd earned every single one of those callouses. "I'll take the dollar tour, if you don't mind putting it on my tab."

"You're running up quite the bill, you know." He seemed pleased by her interest in his home.

"Sue me."

His laughter bounced off the water, not rusty and unused as she would have expected. It was deep and rich and happy to be set free. His straightforward pleasure had the strange effect of making her want to investigate the lake's charm as well.

His hand gently grazed the small of her back and guided her toward the steps of the porch. "When I first started working on the place, I didn't know which end of a hammer to hold."

She studied the roughhewn cedar pillars spaced perfectly along a recently poured cement slab. "You're a fast study."

"Don't look too close. I'm still learning. But I believe a man should always keep learning. Trying new things." He turned. His gaze found hers. "Even when they're uncomfortable." Water lapped against the dock pilings in rhythmic, soothing little waves. "Hungry?"

"Yes."

"Good. I have potatoes baking and steaks marinating for the grill."

"Did the military teach you to be this prepared?"

He shook his head. "I was a boy scout."

"Of course you were." She could almost picture him in his cute little shorts uniform, diligently checking rules off his list. "What can I do to help?"

"Nothing." He pointed to a perfect arrangement of bentwood chairs. "Sit here and keep an eye out that direction."

"What am I looking for?"

"The sunset. It'll be glorious over the water."

J.D. loved to stop for sunsets, but he'd never cooked for her, unless she counted the time he helped the kids make her breakfast in bed one Mother's Day morning. The toaster caught fire. If the Story sisters hadn't come by early that Sunday morning, the parsonage would have gone up in flames.

"I'll preheat the grill." Saul jogged down the steps that led to a large, well-landscaped, stone terrace half-way between the house and the water. Beside the screened-in gazebo sat a shiny, stainless steel grill. "Make yourself at home." He pointed to the chairs on the porch.

Leona started to select a seat that didn't put her in direct eye contact with the water, but as she watched him fiddle with the knobs on the cooker, flashing light flickered behind him and she suddenly changed her mind. Drawn by the beauty, she dropped her sweater over the arm of the chair and placed her shoes and purse at her feet.

Sunlight danced on the tiny ripples stirred by the breeze. West Texas wind was a constant irritation as far as her hair was concerned, but this was the first time she'd witnessed its ability to transform brown-gray water into a field of sparkling diamonds.

The lake wasn't huge, so she could see the line of spindly willow trees hugging the opposite bank. Closer to home, a family of ducks paddled lazily toward Saul's dock and the small boat tethered to a metal cleat. The mother waterfowl craned her neck over her shoulder every few seconds, making sure her little ducks were following in her wake. Oh, how Leona could relate to that poor girl.

"Thirsty?" Saul held out a stemmed glass. She'd been so taken by the scenery she hadn't noticed his return to the porch.

"Lemonade?"

"Fresh-squeezed with a dash of champagne. Made it myself. Brave enough to try it?"

"You're not the only one who believes in trying new things." She took the glass and lifted it to her lips. "Bottoms up."

For the next twenty minutes, Saul carefully finished up dinner and tended the steaks, all the while encouraging her to relax and unwind. She didn't know how to unwind. She hadn't unwound in thirty years. But she gave it her best shot and let her body sink into the cushions while her eyes drank in the serenity. By the time Saul invited her to join him in the gazebo, her legs were jelly. She blamed the loosening of her limbs on the combination of fresh air and alcohol, neither of which she was used to. But as Saul seated her at a small round wrought-iron table inside the gazebo, she thought perhaps she should blame this unsettling contentment upon the man.

His hands resting on the back of her chair, he leaned in and whispered, "There goes the sun."

She looked out across the lake. It was hard to concentrate on the fiery streaks of red and gold slicing through a bank of deep purple clouds with this man's warm breath heating up the back of her neck.

"I love how the colors of the sky are mirrored on the water." He slipped into his chair.

Sitting in a serene world drenched in color, Leona's hand drifted to the warm spot beneath her ear. "God's paintbrush, J.D. used to say," she said softly.

"Indeed." Saul offered her his hand. "Shall we pray?"

She lowered her hand and rested her palm in his. For the first time in all her years of praying she didn't close her eyes. It seemed far more reverent to soak in this divine picture of sky and water, each so different, yet so perfectly matched that the line between them disappeared.

In the quiet approach of evening, she listened for God's voice while a man she barely knew, yet somehow felt as if she'd known forever, spoke reverently to God.

His words to the Creator were like him. Short, direct, and to the point. When he finished his blessing, Saul raised his head and smiled. "Dig in."

Leona spread a cloth napkin across her lap. "So Claire grew up in Texas?"

"No. Her father was a military officer." Saul cut into his meat. "She grew up moving from base to base, as did I." He cut off a perfectly grilled piece. "Unlike me, however, she could always trace her roots back to this place, the land where her great grandfather trapped mustangs on the creek to sell to the Mexican government."

"He must have been quite the cowboy."

"He's buried over by the chimney stack. His stone is one of the few that refuses to submit to the wind." Saul popped the meat in his mouth.

"A stubborn cuss in this life, and beyond."

Saul burst out laughing. "Exactly."

They ate in comfortable silence as the unexpected joy in Saul's deep laugh drifted over the water. Leona wondered if there was more to his wife's family story, but for some reason she was content to let Saul tell it in his own time.

As if he'd sensed her desire to hear more, Saul wiped his mustache. "In the late eighteen hundreds the city wanted to dam up Claire's great grandfather's creek to secure water for the city. That old cuss went to war with the powers that be to fight the injustice, but in the end, as you can see, he lost." Saul pointed his fork toward the graveyard. "According to Claire, legend has it that every time the moon is full, her great grandfather's spirit wanders the lake demanding justice." Saul took a drink of his Mimosa. "I've yet to see him."

"If you did, I think you'd be friends."

"What makes you say that?"

"Justice. It's what usually draws men to the law." She forked the last of her buttery potato to her mouth. "My father had the need to right wrongs. My son has it, too."

"You and J.D. did a fine job with your family."

"Are you admitting that meddling has its place?"

"Claire and I never had children." His wistful tone plucked at Leona's heart. "I had no right to tell you how to raise yours."

An owl hooted in the darkness settling in the cove.

"Tell me about her, please." Did she really want to know about a woman who had come from such impressive stock? Too late now.

"We met on opposing sides of a court martial," Saul perched his silverware on the edge of his empty plate. "By the time she'd finished kicking holes in my airtight case, it was too late. I'd already fallen hopelessly in love with a force to be reckoned with." He drew in a deep breath. "We were both ambitious. Intent on climbing the ranks. I was especially determined not to let our hasty marriage keep me from taking my career by storm or seeing the world."

"You've seen the world?"

"I have."

"There are so many places I want to see."

"You've got the money now."

Why did he always mention the money? Was he the gold digger of David's accusations? "Aren't there places you want to see?"

"I'm content here." He looked at her. "Obviously, you aren't."

Roy's offer, along with his enticing smile popped into her head. "I don't know."

He let his gaze drift to the water. "Three months after Claire and I said I do, we accepted assignments apart. I went abroad as a prosecutor. I saw much of the world while she remained a stateside defender."

"That must have been hard."

Lights that had been strung along the rails of the catwalk leading to the dock suddenly came on. "They're on a sensor." He pushed back from the table and stood. "Shall we dance?"

Realizing he'd taken her as far as he intended on this insightful trip down memory lane, she started stacking the plates. "Shouldn't we clean up first?"

"Dishes can wait. The perfect moment for dancing cannot."

Thinking the man was as layered as an onion and just as difficult to peel, she watched as he dashed up to the porch, snagged her shoes and returned them to her at the gazebo.

The distant strains of a boat motor zipping across the lake buzzed in Leona's ears as she buckled her dance shoes. Saul pulled his dance shoes out from beneath his chair and had them on and laced in a flash. He went to the old fashioned record player sitting beside their table. After lifting the lid, he flipped a switch and set the needle down on the spinning vinyl. "Nothing like a little Cole Porter to channel your inner Fred Astaire."

"I didn't know anyone played vinyl anymore."

"Good dancing requires good music." He held the screen door open. "Hope you've been practicing, Ginger."

Leona looked up from fastening the tiny buckle on her pumps. "Where are we going?"

"The dock."

"Kendra said we shouldn't wear our shoes anywhere but on the dance floor." She did not want to ruin this moment by confessing her fear of water, but her heart was beating so hard against her lungs she could barely breathe. "What if we just push the table back? Make more room in here?"

"You can afford new shoes, Leona." He had her there. "Sun's been down long enough the mosquitos shouldn't be too bad. Besides, the breeze off the water usually keeps them away."

"The water?"

"You haven't danced until you've danced under a full moon reflecting off the water." He nodded toward the orb rising over the roofline of the house. "And tonight's light show promises to be a stunner."

"But what if we fall off the edge?"

He closed the screen door. His shoes padded across the stone. "Are you afraid of water?"

She took a deep breath and lowered her eyes. "I don't swim," she confessed.

He lifted her chin. "And yet, you sat by the lake all evening without saying a word." Compassion in his voice softened the hard knot inside her.

"I've actually enjoyed looking at it." Her eyes rose to his. "For the first time ever."

He lifted his left palm. "Put your hand in mine." The tenderness in his eyes dispelled her caution and compelled her to follow his order. She placed her right hand in his. His arm slipped around her waist. "Trust me."

His left foot slid forward and her right foot slid back. Before she knew it, they were waltzing around the gazebo. "Ready?" he asked as he spun her around.

She kept her eyes locked on his and nodded.

His hold on her secure, Saul pushed the screen door open with his elbow. They waltzed off the stone terrace and danced their way toward the lighted catwalk leading to the dock. He gracefully backed onto the wooden planks, pulling her with him in one easy move. Her breath caught in her throat. With both feet on the boards, she knew now was the moment of commitment. Either she ran for higher ground or she danced on water.

"You're alright." He pulled her closer. His mustache tickled her cheek as he began to whisper in her ear, "Look only at me. Now left. Right. Slide. Together." Eyes locked on his, rather than the water lapping the pilings, she floated across the bridge spanning the water.

By the time they reached the dock's platform, her heart rate was higher than the water level and her breathing so shallow, she could barely sputter, "I can't—"

"You are," he reassured and held her tight against him. "Just dance, Leona."

Strains of Cole Porter's *Let's Do It* cut through the thrum of blood rushing to her head. Saul took the lead, sliding and gliding with the beat. Though she could feel the sway of the dock beneath her feet, she danced with more abandon than if her feet had been on solid ground.

The moon climbed over the trees. *Let's fall in love*, the song repeated over and over.

So she did.

CHAPTER THIRTEEN

Leona had eaten lunch at the Koffee Kup for the second day in a row, hoping to accidentally run into Saul. Granted, she wasn't up on the latest in post-enchanted-evening protocol, but she was beyond caring whether staking out Saul's favorite eating establishment appeared a bit forward. It had been three days since their dance. How long should a woman have to wait to hear from the man who'd turned her world upside down? She checked her phone again. No texts. No missed calls. No word from the man who'd convinced her to dance on water.

She closed *The Intelligent Investor*, snatched her lunch ticket, then headed for the cash register. "The chicken salad was good, Ruthie." She handed over a twenty and waited for the change. "You and Angus are quite the dancers."

"That boy is the best thing that ever happened to me." Ruthie dug in the cash drawer while peering over her glasses at Leona. "Saul's even comin' round to Angus's good points."

The mention of Saul's name sent a flush of heat to Leona's face. She quickly looked away and pretended to be interested in the meringue pies. "Saul been in lately?"

"Me and Angus ain't the only ones who cut a fine rug last Friday night." Ruthie sorted bills and coins into Leona's hand. "You could call him, you know? Finish your business."

"Our business?"

"The *business* of life. 'Bout time you and Saul got on with it, don't you think, Leona?"

Ruthie could read her far better than she read any of her recipes. If Leona didn't change the subject, and quick, Ruthie would zero in on her fear that Saul had not felt what she felt as they danced under that full moon.

Leona stuffed her change into her purse. "I'm so excited for Angus and his college opportunity."

"Lord blessed us, for sure." Ruthie closed the cash drawer with her hip. "Still don't know who to thank, and that financial aid guy ain't tellin' us. You wouldn't have any ideas would you?"

She wished she did. An idea suddenly hit her. What if Howard had made those withdrawals from the Davis checking account to secretly help Angus? Maxine hadn't forgiven Ruthie's grandson for the pot brownie incident so it made sense that Howard wouldn't want to tell her about how he was spending their money.

Leona leaned over the counter and pecked Ruthie's cheek with a kiss. "You're a peach, Ruthie Crouch." She shot out the diner door, anxious to find Maxine and share the possibility she'd been wrong about Howard having a mistress.

Bam. She ran smack into Saul.

"Leona?" His hands cradled her shoulders. His gaze shifted to the investment book she clutched to her chest. A pleased smile crawled out from under his mustache. "Been reading?"

How dare he not call and then tease me like I'm some teenage school girl. "Maybe."

He chuckled and leaned in. "I've missed having you plow into me."

"Have you?" She backed up. "How would I know?"

"You said you needed time."

"Three days?"

He pulled off his sunglasses and gave her a puzzled look. "I know I'm rusty on the dating rules of conduct, but I didn't want to rush you."

Dating? Did he consider that night at his lake house a

date? "You could have at least called to check—"

"Hey, LeLe!"

Leona turned. Roy barreled toward her. "Modyne told me I'd find you here." He wrapped his arm around her waist and planted a kiss on her temple. "I brought you something." He thrust a beautiful coffee table book with Africa in the title at her without even noticing the investment book in her hands. "Want you to see where we're going, get a feel for the adventure you've dreamed of your whole life?"

"Going?" Saul's bewildered gaze quickly morphed into confusion that darted from Leona to Roy and back to Leona.

She tried to discreetly wiggle free before he got the wrong idea, but Roy snugged her tighter, pressing the thick investment book and African picture book into her ribs. "Well, I haven't—"

"Hey, Saul. It is Saul, isn't it?" Roy stuck out his hand, but didn't wait for Saul to respond. "LeLe and I are heading for Africa as soon as I get back from visiting a couple of supporting churches in east Texas, isn't that right, LeLe?"

"Well, like I tried to say—"

"Africa?" Saul's hurt hardened into a daggered glare he hurled Leona's way. "You're flying? Over water, Leona?"

"Of course she is." Roy kissed her temple again. "It's too far to walk and too wet to drive." He chuckled, pleased as a peacock at his joke. "LeLe, I hate to do this to you, darlin', but those fundraising commitments will keep me out of town until Sunday morning. I'm afraid I'll have to miss our dance lessons." Roy spun toward Saul. "My good man, you and LeLe cut a fine rug the other night. Could I impose upon you to give my girl a twirl this Friday night?"

His girl? Leona sputtered, "Maddie's coming home this weekend. I probably won't have time for dancing—"

"Sure you will...*LeLe*." Saul's tone took scissors to her nickname while his steely stare cut straight through her attempt to duck out of this conversation. "I'd be happy to go a couple of rounds on the boards with *your* girl, Roy." Saul shook Roy's hand and before Leona could protest, or defend herself, or explain that she wasn't Roy's girl, Saul announced, "I'll pick you up at eighteen-thirty, *LeLe.* I'm late for court."

"Eighteen-thirty?" Roy asked as they watched Saul double-time it toward the courthouse. "A strange duck, that one."

Leona whirled. "What were you thinking, Roy?"

"That you need a good man to take care of you."

"I can take care of myself."

His dumbfounded look melted into concern. "LeLe, what's wrong?"

She thrust his picture book into his gut. "I haven't agreed to go to Africa. Saul Levy is *not* a strange duck." She hugged her investment book tight. "And I'm perfectly capable of finding my own dance partner."

CHAPTER FOURTEEN

Leona hauled warm clothes from the dryer and deposited them on the couch. Doing laundry felt normal. Something she knew how to do. Something she could do right. And before Maddie walked through the front door, she wanted to feel as if she could do something right because, obviously, she didn't have a clue how to start a new relationship with a man.

"I don't waste time fretting over missing socks." Roxie plopped into one of Leona's new club chairs and helped herself to the Chex mix on the coffee table. "Every time one sock goes missing, it comes back as a Tupperware lid." She tossed a salty square into her mouth.

In no mood to be cheered, Leona moved the bowl of cereal. "That's for the party." She hated feeling this cranky. A first grandchild was supposed to be a happy time for grandparents. Grandparents. Plural. Both of Amy's parents had died before J.D. That left the sole responsibility of grandparenting on Leona's shoulders. Of course, Amy's Aunt Bette Bob would act as a surrogate grandmother, but the truth was, Leona would be walking this journey alone.

She was grateful Roxie had coerced the news out of David. Having someone besides her lawyer to share in her joy helped. "You think the Welcome Home sign on the front porch might be a bit much?"

"Maddie's going to smell a rat when Parker shows up."

"Hence the reason for a party." Leona gathered the small stack of folded towels. "Parker is one of David's dearest friends. Why wouldn't he be invited to their pregnancy reveal?"

"Because David and Amy aren't *revealing* they're pregnant to anyone until Sunday."

"I invited Parker because he's one of David's best friends."

"Hell's bells, Leona." Roxie scooped up another handful of party mix. "You can tell yourself whatever you want." Roxie munched one crunchy piece of cereal at a time as she followed Leona down the hall. "But directing David and Maddie's lives is doing nothing to fix yours."

"He's called. Left messages. Texted." Leona shoved the towels in the cupboard. "I'm not dancing with a man who won't give a person a chance to defend themselves."

"You know where he lives. Why didn't you go make your case?"

Saul's cove was as close to heaven as anything she'd seen in this part of Texas. "The man is…so different than…"

"Roy? Or J.D?" Roxie's ability to hit the nail on the head could be as irritating as comforting.

Leona closed the cabinet door with her hip. "I can't bury another man."

"Then you might as well curl up and die right now because you sure ain't livin', girlfriend."

"Saul has his practice. He's seen the world at war. He has *no* interest in seeing it at peace. He intends to stay in Mt. Hope the rest of his life."

"I don't see you spending your millions traveling the globe."

"Not yet. But I intend to."

"You don't even get your face wet in the shower. How are going to travel over water?"

"Saul implied the same thing." Sweat trickled down her neck. How dare Saul think he knew her simply because she'd balked about dancing on his dock. "Neither of you know what I might do someday."

"Someday?" Roxie snorted. "What if that someday never comes, girlfriend? What if *someday* is right now?"

Tater started barking and scrambled for the front door.

"The kids are here." Leona shook her finger in her friend's face. "Not a word about Saul."

"What if he shows up?"

"I saw his face when he realized I didn't tell him about Africa. He's not coming."

"But he's tried to get ahold of you."

"Probably to tell me he's Ruthie's partner and after he thought it over, he couldn't possibly leave that dear woman high and dry."

"See, he is a gentleman."

Leona shook her finger one more time. "Tonight is not about me."

"It never is." Roxie deflected Leona's glare and zipped her pinched forefinger and thumb across her lips. "Sealed."

"Momma!" Maddie called from the living room.

"Coming!" Leona ran the entire length of the short hall. "Maddie!" She swallowed her beautiful daughter in a thrilled hug. "You're so skinny."

"So are you." Maddie dropped her purse on the couch and held Leona at arm's length for a closer examination. "Have you been exercising?"

"She's dancing," David set Maddie's suitcase on the floor. "With Roy McGee."

"The missionary who used to bring us mangos from Africa?"

"I've had one lesson." Leona didn't mention her dancing practice and she cast a warning reminder Roxie's way to make sure she didn't mention Saul either. "With an old friend."

"Dancing? With an old friend?" Maddie seemed equally surprised and impressed. "What next? Drinking?"

"That too," Roxie quipped.

Why had she told Roxie about the spiked lemonade? "Are you hungry, Maddie?"

"She better be." David surveyed the small living room. "Momma's spread would feed an army."

"Amy's eating for two now." Leona winked at her daughter-in-law.

"Don't blame me for this excess." Amy glowed, her hand resting on her growing midsection.

"Blame Parker." Roxie popped another piece of cereal in her mouth.

Maddie's eyes narrowed. "Parker?"

Leona pulled the plastic wrap off the vegetables and dip. "I thought it would be like old times to include him, tonight."

David's face scrunched into an angry snarl. "Momma, you promised you wouldn't tell anyone our news."

"I haven't told him." Leona dredged a carrot through the

creamy sauce. "You don't have to either. You can do the reveal after he leaves. I just thought your best friend deserved to hear your good news before you announce it to everyone."

David sighed. "You've got a point." He looked at Amy. "What do you think, babe?"

"Tell him." Amy patted her tiny bulge. "Parker's proved he can keep a secret better than anyone in this town. No one knew he was leaving."

"Where's he going?" Maddie's antenna shot up despite her best efforts to act uninterested, which pleased Leona immensely.

"Guatemala." David reached for a piece of celery.

"Another mission trip?" Maddie asked.

David poked a piece of celery in the dip. "Permanent change of residence."

Maddie's face sobered for a second and then quickly recovered. "He always said he wanted to go." She smiled. "Good for him."

Unwilling to believe Maddie was genuinely happy to hear Parker was living his dream without her, Leona glanced out the window. "You can tell him yourself, Maddie. He just pulled in the drive."

"Momma—"

Roxie interrupted Maddie's protest. "Leona, why don't

David and I let Parker in while you and Amy give Maddie a tour of your new house?" Roxie wiped her hands on her skinny jeans.

"Great idea." Leona picked up Maddie's bag. "That'll give Maddie a chance to freshen up from her long flight."

Maddie rolled her eyes at Amy. "Momma's house may be different, but her inability to stay out of my life hasn't changed a bit."

"Lucky you." Amy grabbed Maddie's bag.

"I'll carry that." Maddie relieved Amy of the bag. "Sorry, Amy."

"Your Momma means well," Amy chided, looping her arm through Maddie's.

"Don't tell me she's growing on you."

"I heard that." Leona couldn't help but smile at the sound of their laughter. Moving out and giving Amy space had advanced their relationship. Now, to move in and set to work on her plan for Maddie.

The girls followed Leona down the hall and into the freshly painted bedroom. "I barely got the place put together in time for your arrival." Leona closed the door.

"No pink?" Maddie's edgy tone meant the conversation about Parker wasn't over.

"No beige either."

Maddie set her bag on a chair next to a table with a reading lamp. "Did you bring me home because Parker is leaving?"

"What can it hurt to tell him goodbye?"

"I know you mean well, but let me say this as gently as possible. I'm not going to marry, at least not any time soon. Maybe never. Parker's a great guy, but we want different things."

Leona eased onto the bed. "Girls." She patted the empty space on either side of her, inviting Maddie and Amy to join her. "Amy, tell her how nice it is to have someone to come home to."

"I don't think I want to be in the middle of this." Amy started to rise and Leona grabbed her hand.

"But Amy has made time for David, a career, and now, a baby." Leona pulled Amy back to the bed. "It is possible to have it all, Maddie."

"Momma, you loved Daddy. You spent the last thirty years raising me and David. All of that's gone now. I think you're projecting your loneliness on me." Stung by truth for the second time in five minutes. Was the Lord trying to tell her something? "So, it might be fun hanging out with a fellow who looks like Crocodile Dundee and keeps you stocked in dried mangos."

"She's got a point, Leona," Amy said, getting even for being forced into their feud.

Leona shot an exasperated look at Amy. "Roy's an old friend."

"Who's asked her to go to Africa," Amy added.

"Really?" Maddie's eyes sparkled with the possibility that she'd stumbled upon the key to diverting this conversation. "I think you should be wicked and go, Momma."

"You can't get rid of me that easily."

Maddie kissed her cheek. "I know, but it was worth a shot."

"Momma!" David knocked on the door then stuck his head in. "Your dancing partner is here."

Maddie jumped off the bed. "I haven't seen Roy in years."

"It's not Roy." David didn't hide his displeasure. "Care to explain why Saul Levy's here looking like your prom date, Momma?"

"Ugh." Leona's shoulders sagged. "Tell him I'm not going tonight."

David came in and closed the door behind him. "The less I say to that sawed-off shotgun, the better."

"Saul Levy?" Maddie's grin took on a mischievous slant. "Momma's dating two men at the same time?"

"It's not what y'all are thinking."

"I hope not, Momma," David said. "Saul Levy is a jerk."

The man who'd waltzed her around the lake was in no way a jerk. Leona stood and smoothed her skirt. "Who I choose to dance with is none of your business."

"My point exactly." Maddie crossed her arms. "It's miserable when someone's trying to tell you how to live your life, isn't it?"

Leona yanked the bedroom door open and stormed down the hall. She marched into the cluster of Saul, Roxie, and Parker and extended her right hand. "Saul, I'm sorry we failed to connect this week."

He took her hand and held on. "The failure is all mine."

That he'd taken the blame for her refusal to talk set Leona back a few beats. "Maddie came into town for the weekend. We're having a little family party tonight. I'll have to miss our dance lesson. Sorry for the misunderstanding." She squeezed his hand in hopes he would somehow know she meant her regret had nothing to do with dance lessons.

He smiled at her, a warm forgiving smile that said they'd never been enemies in his eyes. "Sometimes wires get crossed."

Crossed was an understatement? She'd allowed the court of public opinion, of which her children were judge and jury, to twist more than the thin wire connecting her to this man. Her emotions were so knotted it would take years to completely unravel them. Years she didn't want to waste worrying about what others thought.

Casting reason aside, Leona smiled and said, "Then I say it's time to uncross them." She threw her arms around Saul and gave him a big hug. To her relief, he hugged her back. When she pulled away, his expression leaned more toward charmed amusement than surprise. "I'd love for you to join us, Mr. Levy."

"It would be my pleasure, Mrs. Harper."

Leona didn't have to glance over her shoulder to know David and Maddie's mouths were hanging ajar.

CHAPTER FIFTEEN

Roxie pulled Leona into the kitchen and crowed, "That's what I'm talkin' about, girlfriend." She held her palm up for a high-five, which Leona purposely ignored.

"What in the world made me think inviting Saul to stay was a good idea?" Leona slumped against the wall and dropped her head into her hands.

"Nothing else matters—" Roxie lifted her chin. "—when you're in love, my friend."

Love? Even when she was young and giddy and falling in love with J.D., she'd never counted butterfly stirrings in her belly as love. Whenever she was around Roy, it was more like the time some rude boys pushed her into the camp lake and she thought she was drowning. Saul was what it felt like when her feet finally found the shore. Saul was solid ground.

"I don't think so, Roxie."

"David will come around."

"He called him a sawed-off shotgun."

"To his face?"

"No." At least she hoped Saul hadn't heard their discussion. "They've been at odds since we discovered J.D.'s will. David thinks Saul is after my money!"

Roxie led Leona to one of her new kitchenette stools. "David loved his daddy. J.D.'s secret hurt him. He's got to blame somebody." She wiggled her tight jeans aboard the opposite stool. "Your son also loves you, Leona. Give him a minute or two. David wants you to be happy and once he calms down, he'll see what I see."

"A foolish old woman?"

"A woman whose eyes are finally beginning to sparkle again."

"Momma?" Maddie stuck her head in the kitchen. "We need a referee."

"Here we go." Leona snatched a tray of little sandwiches from the fridge. "If I can keep their mouths full of chicken salad maybe I can keep them from eating each other."

She waltzed into the living room just as David asked Saul, "What do you mean, Dad helped you renovate your lake house?"

"I'd been living in my RV for a while. J.D. thought I'd feel more settled if I could move into the house. So he offered to help me pour the porch slab," Saul said.

Leona froze. "When?"

Saul's face sobered. He took a deep breath and said, "A few days before he died."

Now, no one moved. The sandwich tray grew heavier and heavier in Leona's hands. Had the physical exertion added to J.D.'s stress and contributed to his heart attack?

She swallowed. "I guess I didn't know you and J.D. were more than lawyer and client, pastor and occasional parishioner."

Saul's eyes pleaded with her to understand. "We were friends."

"And so you think that gives you the right to make a move on his wife?"

"James David!" Leona set the tray down. "That's enough."

"I'm sorry, Momma." David snagged Amy's hand. "We better go." He stopped in front of Saul. "I apologize, Mr. Levy. I'm obviously very protective when it comes to my mother."

"As a good son should be."

David and Amy left. Leona wanted to go after them to assure David he wasn't the only one blindsided by the revelation.

"Maddie," Roxie's voice broke the awkward silence. "Why don't you and Parker come help me tidy up the kitchen?" Roxie picked up the sandwich tray and Maddie and Parker didn't just follow her out, they ran out, leaving Leona and Saul to face each other alone.

Leona didn't know why she felt the need to fix this. After all, this revelation was one more painful reminder she hadn't known her husband as intimately as she'd always thought. "David may be his father's son, but he inherited my temper."

Saul offered a forgiving chuckle, which had the surprising effect of eliciting a laugh from her. It wasn't Saul's responsibility to keep her in the loop of her husband's friendships. It was J.D. she was still mad at.

She waved toward the couch. "Care to sit?"

He nodded and sat opposite her. For a moment, neither of them spoke.

"I didn't know you and J.D. hung out."

"I assumed you knew your husband was fishing off my dock or helping me restore the cabin."

"Finding out you didn't know everything about the man you thought you knew better than yourself is ..."

"Unsettling?"

She nodded. "What did you talk about?" She stopped his protest with a raised finger. "Don't think you're going to get away with claiming that lawyer-client privilege stuff."

A smile lifted his mustache. "Politics. Religion. The weather." His gaze tangled with hers. "Everything."

"Me?"

"He worried about you."

"Because I'd never done anything on my own?"

"He knew you'd sacrificed a lot to become a pastor's wife. Your career. Financial security. Travel. The privacy you craved. J.D. wanted to make certain you knew how much he counted on you, appreciated everything you did, and wanted you to have what you needed to start over...if anything happened to him before he had the chance to tell you personally."

"He had thirty years to tell me."

"But he showed you every day, didn't he?"

Gas in her van. Plumbing repairs made on his day off. Her computer mistakes salvaged. Saul was right. J.D.'s way with words shined brightest in the pulpit, but his ability to show love resonated in simple everyday actions. "And so the two of you planned the reinvention of Leona Harper?"

"I promised him I'd carry out his wishes."

"J.D. didn't think I could take care of myself?"

"Just the opposite. And now that I've gotten to know you, I see why." Saul rubbed his palms, the friction audible. "My wife was a wonderful woman, in every way. I've not admired another woman as I did her … until now." Saul gaze was trained on hers. "I've spent my life being prepared for anything, as well as helping others do the same. But I wasn't prepared…"

Leona's heart tripped. Is this where he told her that she and her family were crazy? That he wanted no part of her reinvention or spending Sunday afternoons grilling steaks at the lake or practicing their dance moves on moonlit docks…she made her mind stop running ahead.

Something told her not to say another word. To wait. Patiently.

Saul stopped rubbing his palms. "But I wasn't' prepared for falling in love with you," he whispered as he reached for her hand. His thumb gently grazed her knuckles. "If wanting to dance with you forever is making a move on you, then I'm guilty as charged."

In love?

While the faint strains of *Let's Fall in Love* played in her head, the picture of David's pained face flashed in her eyes. What was she doing? She had no business falling in love with anyone, much less someone her son couldn't stand to be in the same room with.

"Grief can do strange things to our memories. Make things

seem worse than they were." She pulled free of Saul's gentle caress. "It's time I stop looking at yesterday through today's lens."

Saul's brow knit in confusion. "What does that mean?"

"Even if J.D. hadn't left me a dime, he left me a lifetime of memories. Being alone is hard. Harder than anything I've ever done. I think I've been filtering past memories through my current pain. Grief makes it harder to remember the good." She rubbed the tiny stone of her wedding ring. "Truth is, J.D. and I had a wonderful marriage and a wonderful life. We trusted each other. He wasn't trying to hurt me by keeping his investments a secret, was he?"

"He believed you to be a woman more than capable of standing on her own two feet."

"Thank you." Tears stung her eyes. "I don't think I realized, until now, how much J.D. loved me ... and ..." Elephant-sized grief plopped on her chest, making it almost impossible to breathe.

"And how much you still love him." The lack of judgment in Saul's tone was a balm to her soul, but the sadness in his eyes broke her heart.

She gave a conflicted nod. "I'm sorry, Saul."

CHAPTER SIXTEEN

Leona read Maddie's note again.

Helping Parker at his ranch. Will meet you at parsonage later.

A weary smile lifted Leona's lip. At least her children were going to be happy.

Her conversation with Saul had robbed her of more than a decent night's sleep. The possibility she could love two men at the same time had stolen her peace. She may have told Saul she couldn't love him because she was still in love with J.D., but that wasn't true. She did love him.

Leona glanced at the clock. Moping wouldn't change things for her and it sure wouldn't get David and Amy's nursery painted. She poured her coffee in the sink and gathered her paint supplies. Something about dragging fresh paint over marred walls always helped her see things with a fresh perspective. Besides, the time spent with her kids would give her an opportunity to reassure David that he didn't have to worry about her choosing Saul over his father. She had her love life under control … even if one man was dead and she'd killed the other with a simple *I'm sorry*.

She loaded everything into the van and climbed into the driver's seat. The turn of the key produced a click as dead as her heart. She tried again. And again. Same sickening click.

"Not today." She dug her phone out of her purse and called the church. "Shirley, is Cotton there?"

"He's cruising the Mediterranean with your mother, remember?"

"Ugh. I forgot." Leona tapped the wheel. "What about David?"

"He said he needed to clear his head."

"He went fishing, didn't he?" Hopefully, he wasn't trolling past Saul's lake house with plans to egg the place. "Did he say when he'd be back?"

"That boy is like his father when it comes to fishing. Stays as long as it takes to puzzle over whatever issue is troubling him."

"That could take until sunset."

Shirley must have heard the distress in Leona's voice

because she asked, "Everything okay?"

"My car won't start. I told Amy that Maddie and I would come paint the ..." Leona caught herself before spilling the beans.

"Nursery?"

"You didn't hear it from me."

"Didn't have to. I have eyes. Amy's tummy is not as flat as it used to be. Reckon David's puzzling on being a father?"

"Probably." Shirley was good as gold, but Leona wasn't in a mood to tell her that her interest in Saul Levy had sent David to the lake. Her ex-interest, Leona clarified in her head. "Would you mind giving me a lift, Shirley?"

"I'd be happy to help, but the baptistry is making that strange gurgling sound again. David asked if I could come by on my day off and let the plumber in. Hey, I know. Call Etta May and Nola Gay. They've got that Uber service now, you know? Probably give you the pastor's rate."

Leona hung up knowing her move to the other side of town hadn't taken her as far from the life she knew as she might have hoped. *Hoped?* Was she really wanting to move on? To let go of her former life? To let go of J.D.? She had some puzzling of her own to do and painting was the perfect medium.

A few rings later, she'd nervously launched the excited

Story twins into action. Leona hauled two cans of paint, several brushes, a couple of rollers, and a few disposable paint trays out of the van and waited on the curb.

She heard the big blue van a few seconds before she saw the cloud of smoke that trailed the lumbering vehicle. The van screeched to a stop. Loud country music shook the vehicle's closed windows and vibrated Leona's chest.

Nola Gay rolled down the window. "You're our first customer, Leona," she shouted over *I've Got Friends in Low Places*.

"Lord, help me," Leona muttered as she loaded her stuff into the back and climbed through the sliding door Etta May had shouldered open. "What's that smell?" Leona sniffed as she dropped into the bucket seat covered with a crocheted throw.

"Mountain Essence carpet deodorizer." Etta May shouted over the rattle of the motor and thrum of the music. "Keeps this pretty shag smelling fresh as a daisy." She ran her hand over the flattened nap of the gold-toned carpet. "You should've seen it before we rented a shampooer. We haven't figured out how we're going to tidy up that ceiling." She pointed to the purple fake fur headliner. "Don't worry, though. We think we vacuumed out most of the bugs."

"You know what?" Leona started to climb out. "I don't feel

up to painting today."

Etta May shoved her back in. "Bluebird here may not be much to look at, but she rides—"

"Bluebird?" Leona asked, regretting showing interest the minute the word left her gaping mouth.

Etta May popped the van's roof. "We named her that because she flies like she has wings." She heaved the door shut in Leona's face.

Leona lunged for the handle, which was useless because there wasn't one.

Etta May hopped into the passenger seat. "Belt up, Leona. We can't afford another hike in our insurance premiums." She clicked in and patted Nola Gay on the shoulder. "Hit it, sister."

While Leona was fumbling around for the clasp to secure her seatbelt, Nola Gay floored the gas and Bluebird peeled out, leaving a trail of rubber that would be a permanent reminder of this bad decision.

"I'm not in a hurry," Leona shouted over the blare of Garth's reminder of how low she'd sunk. At the stop sign, Nola Gay barely slowed then cranked a hard right. "Where are you going, Nola Gay?"

"I don't know, but we're making good time," Nola shouted back, her hands wrestling the shimmy of the steering wheel.

Leona's nails dug into Etta May's seat. "The parsonage is

the other way," she shouted.

"I think she's right, sister," Etta May agreed.

"Well, pickle my gizzard." Nola Gay did a quick glance in her mirrors. "Hang on, y'all." She whipped a U-turn in the middle of the street.

Leona braced her arms against the seats as her life flashed before her eyes. "Lord, help us."

Nola Gay goosed the gas and Bluebird flew down Main. They zipped past the Mt. Hope Messenger, the Koffee Kup café, and Dewey's Hardware.

"It's red." Etta May screamed as she pointed to the town's lone stoplight swinging in the wind.

Nola Gay stomped the brake. Leona's seatbelt tightened. They fishtailed to a stop half-way through the intersection.

Pleased at her successful handling of Bluebird, Nola Gay glanced over her shoulder, "Good thing the auction barn's closed today. Main can get pretty jammed up with all those pickups and overloaded stock trailers."

Leona's trembling hands unhooked her seatbelt. "I can walk from here."

"We charged you door to door, Leona." Nola Gay stomped the gas again and they shot through the intersection. "Door to door it is."

Three minutes later, they screeched to a halt in the

parsonage driveway. Leona's legs were so wobbly she could hardly manage the porch steps. She'd tried talking the twins out of helping her carry her load into the house, but they'd insisted their services included both fetching and toting.

"Hey, Amy." Nola Gay held up a paint can. "Blessed Blue. Something you want to tell us?"

Amy's wide eyes darted to Leona. "Not really." She reluctantly opened the screen.

"We know the only color Maxine allows in the parsonage is beige." Nola Gay hiked her skirt and trudged up the steps. "Except when it comes to the *children's* rooms."

"Maxine claims the exception to the rule proves she has a heart." Etta May huffed onto the porch with a paint can and the roller tray. "So when's this baby due?"

Leona dropped her supplies and quickly began gathering supplies from the hands of the Story sisters. "Well, thanks for the ride. Y'all be safe on your drive home."

"We're not going anywhere." Nola Gay refused to release her hold on the paint can. "Our motto is: *Dance with the one that brung ya!* See." She pointed toward the van and, sure enough, the hand-lettered saying ran the entire length of the vehicle. "Printed right in plain sight." Nola Gay peeled Leona's hand from the paint can handle. "We brought you. We take you home." She charged through the open screen door.

Amy stopped Leona's argument with the palm of her hand. "I'll make ice tea."

"You don't need to wait on us in your *condition*, dear," Etta May said as she followed her sister. "We know our way around the kitchen."

"I didn't say a word," Leona whispered to Amy.

Amy shook her head. "Nothing's secret in this town."

Leona's conversation with Saul pressed into her thoughts. How many people had seen her making a fool of herself over that man? "The twins have a sixth sense about them that's scary."

"Come on." Amy smiled and looped her arm through Leona's. "I can't wait to see this color on the walls."

For the next couple of hours, Leona rolled Blessed Blue over navy walls and silver Dallas Cowboy stars. Each swipe buried another chunk of her life.

"It's looking so good." Amy handed her a fresh glass of tea. "Thanks for using your day off to help me."

Leona let a big gulp of the sweetness slide down her throat. "You look tired."

"Feeling a little nauseated."

"Kind of late in the day for morning sickness, isn't it?"

"Yeah, I thought I was pretty much past the queasy stage."

"Maybe it's the paint fumes?"

"I chose this paint because it's safe for pregnant mothers."

"Okay." Leona didn't like how the rosiness was slipping from Amy's cheeks. "I'd feel better if you sat for a few minutes. Maybe check your sugar again."

"You sound like David."

"I know you're the nurse, but—"

"I'm being careful and I'm not helpless." Amy waved her off. "I can cut in around the baseboards."

Leona gathered her courage and pressed on. "I'm sorry I didn't seem excited the night you told me about the baby. It scared me. For you, and the baby."

"I think David's a little scared too."

"He loves you."

"I know."

"He can't wait to be a father. And I can't wait to be a grandmother." She hugged Amy. "Making sure the people we love are cared for is what family does."

"Sometimes, family's help can be more of a hindrance."

Leona wasn't sure where Amy was going with this so she kept her questions to herself and took another sip of tea.

"David loved his father. Misses him every time he steps into that church building or walks into this house. When you left, it was like he lost you too."

The revelation was a gut punch. "No wonder he's hurting."

"He wants you to be happy. To have your own life. He knows people can't choose who they love." Amy sat on the rung of the stepladder. "Not even you."

"J.D. Harper was the love of my life."

"Was," Amy said softly. "Saul Levy's brought the sparkle back to your eyes."

A light rap on the doorframe ended their conversation. "Leona?" Maxine stepped into the room with a caution that made Leona regret she'd let so much time pass without checking on the woman.

Leona suddenly remembered that she'd intended to invite Maxine to help, but she'd been so wrapped up in her own problems she'd completely pushed Maxine's troubles aside. "Maxine, I should have—"

"Hope you don't mind me letting myself in, Amy, but the door was open and I didn't want to wake those nosy Story sisters."

Amy let out a resigned sigh. "No problem, Maxine."

"Nice color." The compliment was as unusual as the pale color of Maxine's face.

"The room needed to be freshened," Leona said, not wanting Maxine to put two and two together and guess about the baby before David had a chance to make the big announcement.

"Paint it whatever color you want," Maxine's deadpan tone jarred Leona to the core.

"Are you okay, Maxine?"

"Could we talk? In private? Maybe on the porch?"

"Sure." Leona stepped over the paint tray, wondering if she was stepping into a hidden bear trap. "Eat something," she whispered to Amy. "And stay off that ladder."

She followed Maxine down the stairs and past the two Story sisters who were sleeping with their heads resting on the back of the couch, their feet propped on the coffee table, and their mouths hanging open.

Once they were on the porch, Maxine pulled Leona to the far end. "Have you had a chance to ask Saul about being my lawyer?"

"No," Leona confessed.

"Why not?"

"Because once you go down that road it's almost impossible to turn back."

"Howard and I have been fighting for years."

"What do you fight about?"

"Anything that comes up."

"Have you thought about talking to a counselor?"

"When you lose someone you love, it forever changes the way you look at the world."

"Yes, it does." Leona's heart clenched. "But a counselor can help you find a way to keep living."

"Not everyone has your faith, Leona."

If Maxine only knew how she struggled. "I refuse to believe you're a lost cause."

"Counseling is not going to bring my son back. Howard and I are broken beyond repair."

"If not counseling, then before you throw away thirty years with a man you still love, please consider getting to the bottom of what's going on with Howard."

"Just speak to Saul, please."

Leona sighed. "If you're so set on going through with this without giving Howard a chance to explain, you're going to have to ask Saul yourself."

"He's looked at me funny ever since the night you and I … had that unfortunate encounter with that pan of pot brownies." She crossed her arms. "I don't think he likes me."

"You weren't the only one high."

"In Saul's eyes, all's forgiven as far as you're concerned. I've seen how he looks at you."

Who else had picked up on the connection between her and Saul? "I don't think Saul bases his legal representation on whether or not he likes someone." At least, she hoped not. She still needed his legal help and she hoped once their emotions cooled, they could resume their business relationship. "I can't ask him to end your marriage in good conscience, Maxine."

Maxine stiffened into the formidable force Leona suspected Howard was tired of dealing with. "Well, if you don't ask him, I'll see to it that David and Amy don't have a nest for that little one."

"What little one?"

"Don't play dumb with me. I know nursery paint when I see it."

The sensation of living in a glass house was a fire sweeping through her. She was tired of fending off the rocks this woman hurled. "Are you threatening me, Maxine?"

"Call it whatever you want."

"You know, Maxine. You can take this parsonage and shove it where the sun don't shine."

Maxine's eyes grew wide. "You're inability to control your mouth is the direct result of fraternizing with that redheaded Episcopalian." The jab at Roxie popped Leona's cork.

"I could buy this parsonage ten times over if I wanted." Her secret bubbled out like hot lava. "I'm rich, Maxine. Richer than you and Howard ever dreamed of being."

Maxine stepped back as if Leona had hauled off and slapped her. "How on earth?"

"Let me just tell you, my nest egg didn't come from that paltry salary you paid my husband all those years."

"Your mother, then?"

"Bertie had nothing to do—" Leona's rant was cut short by a loud crash from inside the house. "Oh no." She left Maxine on the porch and shot inside. "Amy!"

The Story sisters stirred as she raced past. "What was that, Leona?" Nola Gay rubbed at her eyes.

"I don't know." Terror drove Leona up the stairs two at a time. "Amy!" She burst into the nursery. "Amy!"

Her daughter-in-law lay on the floor. Paint puddled around the turned-over paint can at her feet. "Amy!" Leona knelt beside the pale blonde and hollered, "Etta May! Call Charlie. We need an ambulance."

Maxine burst into the room. "What happened?"

"Call David!" Leona ordered, fear pounding in her ears. "Amy?" She shook Amy's shoulder, relieved when the girl opened her eyes. "Amy? Can you hear me?"

"Uh…"

"What happened?"

"I'm gonna be sick," Amy mumbled.

Leona hooked her arms under Amy's and lifted her to a sitting position. Amy immediately vomited. "Where's that ambulance?" Leona shouted.

"David's not answering," Maxine said.

"He's on the lake. Probably in a cove without service." Or he didn't want to deal with Maxine today and declined her call when he saw the caller ID. Leona's mind raced. She tossed Maxine her phone. "Try again. If he doesn't answer, call Saul. Tell him I need David off the lake. Now."

Etta May huffed into the room. "Charlie's ambulance is in the shop. He said he could bring his son's pickup but it's chock full of roofing supplies."

Amy vomited again.

"Oh, baby." Leona handed her a clean paint rag. "I think your sugar is off."

"Who are you?" Amy asked.

Leona's heart beat against her chest. "Amy, how do I check your sugar?"

"I'm not your sugar, sweetie pie," Amy mumbled.

"That's it." Leona scrambled to her feet. "Etta May, tell Nola Gay to fire up Bluebird. We've got to get this girl to the hospital." Etta May just stood there, her mouth hanging open. "Now!"

Etta May shot out of the room. "Emergency! Emergency, Nola Gay."

"Couldn't get David." Maxine handed Leona her phone. "But Saul answered your call on the first ring. He's on his way to the lake."

Leona reached down to lift Amy to her feet. "Help me get her to the van, Maxine."

"Get your hands off me." Amy's hands pawed at Leona. Her hands smacked the paint puddle. Splatters nailed Leona's face and clothes. Amy stared at her paint-covered hands. "I've got to get my nails done."

"Is she delusional?" Maxine asked.

"Yes!" Painting dripping off her nose, Leona captured Amy's hands.

"Why?"

"Because she's nineteen weeks pregnant and heading for a diabetic catastrophe." Leona draped Amy's arm around her shoulder. "Happy now?"

"She shouldn't have been painting."

If her hands hadn't been full, Leona would have grabbed Maxine by the shoulders and shook her. "Are you going to preach at me or help me?"

"Now you know how it feels to be in trouble."

"You can say I told you so all the way to the hospital."

"See why Howard left me?" Maxine draped Amy's other arm around her neck. "I'm awful."

CHAPTER SEVENTEEN

"Try Maddie again," Leona shouted over the blare of Nola Gay laying on the horn as Bluebird sailed through the red light. Brakes screeched from every direction.

"It's not my fault your children don't want to speak to you, Leona." Maxine tapped Maddie's number again. "I think Amy just passed out."

Leona caught Amy's slumped body and yelled. "Punch it, Nola Gay."

Minutes later, Nola Gay palmed the horn as they careened under the ER's portico cache and ground to a jarring halt.

Maxine pounded the van's sliding door. "Let me out of this death trap." The second Etta May pried the door open, Maxine jumped out. "Going after help."

Leona stroked Amy's damp curls and continued the

prayers she'd been sending up on their wild ride. "Lord, I love this sweet girl. Protect her and my grandbaby."

Maxine returned with two nurses and a gurney. They loaded Amy. As they whisked her away, Leona shouted, "I love you."

"Come on," Maxine wrapped her arm around Leona's shoulder. "Let's get you cleaned up."

"I can't leave."

She inclined her head toward the small bathroom. "I'll knock on the door if they come back with any news."

"I didn't grab my purse. I don't even have a comb."

Maxine patted the bag slung over her shoulder. "Good thing I'm your thorn in the flesh."

Five minutes later, Leona emerged with hair dripping and shirt damp from scrubbing at the splatters, but the terror of losing her daughter-in-law and grandbaby clung to her like dried paint.

Maxine held out a hot cup of vending machine coffee. "The Story girls parked themselves over there."

Leona gave Maxine her comb. "Any news from David?"

Maxine shook her head and led Leona to an empty chair next to Etta May.

Nola Gay leaned over and patted Leona's leg. "We've been praying our fool heads off, Leona."

"Want us to fire up the prayer chain?" Etta May asked.

Risking David's ire over letting their secret out, Leona nodded. "Sounds like a good idea."

Etta May whipped out her phone and started texting like a pro.

Leona's phone buzzed. "Maddie. I think Amy's sugar got off kilter. We're at the hospital." She went on to give details as Maddie and Parker jumped in his truck and sped from his small ranch to town. David buzzed in and she switched over. "David. Where are you?"

"I'm with Saul. We're almost there." David's voice cracked. "How are they?"

"We haven't heard from the doctor."

"Do we need to Care Flight Amy to Dallas?"

"Maddie's on her way. Let's wait for her, okay?"

Fifteen minutes later, David and Maddie hit the emergency room doors at the same time. Maddie was trailed by Parker and David was trailed by Saul. Leona had never been so glad to see someone in her life.

"Update us, Momma," Maddie said.

"Her sugar is high. Around 600." Leona caught the flash of concern in Maddie's eyes. "They're giving her IV fluids and insulin."

"Can I see her?" David asked.

"She's awake and coherent enough to be asking for you." Leona squeezed his hand and he shot through the swinging doors. She and Maddie immediately embraced. "Tell me they're going to be alright."

"I'd feel better if she had a maternal-fetal specialist here." Maddie realized the obvious observation had not been comforting. "Don't worry, Momma. It's good that she's talking and making sense."

"Why are they're keeping her in ICU for a couple of days?" Leona asked.

"Observation. Precaution. It's a good thing. Want me to go see what I can find out?"

Leona nodded. "I should have insisted she teach me what to do in a sugar crisis. It's so hard to know when to meddle and when to back off."

Maddie took her by the shoulders. "I can't believe I'm going to say this, but this time your meddling saved Amy's life." She hugged Leona then slipped through the swinging doors.

Leona turned to see Saul standing a few feet away. Even though it was Saturday, he was wearing his customary creased suit pants, but no jacket or tie. The sleeves on his white shirt were rolled to the elbow. Sweat rings bled from under his arms and muddy water splats covered his shiny shoes. Obviously, he'd hopped into his boat and sped across the lake. And he'd done it to help her. Empathy swam in his eyes, but he kept a respectful distance.

Resisting the urge to throw herself into his arms, she walked to him and extended her right hand. "Thank you."

His touch was a piece of solid ground. "Amy going to be alright?"

"She's feeling a lot better." Tears sprouted and she collapsed into his arms. "We could have lost them," she sobbed.

Saul's arm slid around her waist and held her with the same reassuring strength he'd offered on the night they'd danced on the dock. "But you didn't."

She was greedily soaking in the support when someone behind her cleared their throat. A sudden awareness of several pairs of curious eyes caused Leona to push back from Saul's chest. "You're right. We didn't." A pale swath of Blessed Blue covered Saul's shoulder. She accepted the pressed handkerchief he offered and dabbed at the mess. "I think I owe you a new shirt."

Saul glanced at her futile attempts to clean him up and chuckled. "I'll add it to your bill."

Maxine cleared her throat again. "It seems the crisis has passed."

"It does." Leona hugged her. "Thanks for your help. Maybe the Storys can take you back to your car."

"How will you get home?" Maxine asked.

"I'm happy to take her," Saul offered.

"I've imposed enough for—"

Saul shut down Leona's protest. "No imposition at all."

Maxine smiled. "Thank you, Mr. Levy." To Leona, she said, "I'll clean up the mess in the parsonage if you'll help me clean up the little mess we were discussing earlier." Her eyes cut between Leona and Saul with a definite talk-to-him message.

Before Leona could protest, Maxine had the Story sisters marching toward the door. She reassured them that she might not be as rich as Leona but she could afford to pay both hers and Leona's fares.

"Rich?" Etta May said. "Leona's rich?"

"I guess we gave her the pastor's discount for nothing," Nola muttered.

"What was that about?" Saul asked once the ER doors slid shut.

"In a moment of provocation, I may have let it slip about my financial situation."

"I thought you didn't want anyone to know."

"I don't."

"Then why did you do it?"

"Since I was two, I've done what everyone wanted me to do. Guess I've finally had enough."

"Obligation is a heavy burden." His statement was neither praise nor judgment, but it felt just right. "Have you had dinner?"

"Haven't eaten since breakfast."

Saul turned to Parker. "Can you give Maddie a ride home?"

"You bet." Parker jumped on the opportunity to spend more time with Maddie with such enthusiasm that Leona wondered if her plan to bring Maddie home was working out after all.

"I should stay."

Saul's brow rose. "Should?"

"I *want* to check on the kids."

"Take your time."

When Leona entered her daughter-in-law's room, she was thrilled to see Amy sitting up and the color back in her cheeks. "And the baby?" she asked.

"Fine." Maddie pointed to the ultrasound pic up on the screen.

Leona couldn't contain the tears. "A boy?"

"Little J.D. and his momma are doing great thanks to you, Momma." David hooked his arm around her shoulder.

"J.D.?" Leona asked.

"The Third." Amy held out her hand. "You saved our lives."

Leona's heart was near bursting. "Need anything?"

"We're good," Amy said.

"I think I'll let you celebrate alone." Leona started to leave. "Maddie, Parker's still out there. Should I send him on or do you want him to give you a ride home?"

"I hate to make him hang around when he's got so much to do to get ready for his move," Maddie said. "Are the Storys still here?"

Disappointed Maddie's enthusiasm didn't match Parker's, Leona said, "Sent them home."

"How are you getting home?" David asked.

She stiffened. "Saul's offered dinner and a ride whenever I'm ready."

"Great." David smiled. "But if he offers you a ride in his boat, strap in because that good man drives like a bat out of hell. No wonder Dad liked him."

Good man? "You know how I am about water."

"You know how I am about my momma." That was a close to saying I'm sorry as David was going to come, but it was close enough to send her dancing down the hall.

CHAPTER EIGHTEEN

Tater howled at the rattling screen door.

"Hang on, Maddie." Leona rushed through the living room, tying her robe as she went, and smiling that Maddie and Parker had spent some more time together. "Sorry, I locked you out." She yanked open the door.

"Hey, LeLe." Roy leaned on her doorframe. "You wouldn't happen to have a cup of coffee for a weary traveler?"

"Roy?" Leona gathered the collar on her robe. "I thought you weren't coming back until tomorrow."

He slapped his hand against his chest in a dramatic show of hurt. "Not exactly the welcome I was hopin' for."

"I'm a little worn out."

"It was a joke, LeLe."

"Oh."

"Can I come in?" He kissed her cheek then pressed past her. His bulk filled the room but not the loneliness she'd felt since Saul dropped her off. "David called and asked if I could come back early and fill the pulpit for him tomorrow. He didn't say what was wrong, but he sure sounded upset."

"Amy had a little … medical crisis today, but everyone's fine."

"Everyone?"

She stood there, hand clasping her robe, weighing how much to say and wishing the Lord would give her the best way to say it. "You might as well know. Everyone else does." Leona headed for the kitchen and flipped on the Keurig.

"Know what?" Roy trailed her.

"Amy's pregnant."

Roy's grin split his tan face. "Well, congratulations, Grandma."

Leona disliked his twangy version of *Grandma* almost as much as she disliked being called LeLe. "Amy is going to have a difficult pregnancy. So…"

He pulled out a stool at the table and sat down. "So?"

"So, I'm afraid I'm going to have to decline your invitation to go to Africa."

He leaned forward with a conspiratorial grin, like he hadn't believed her. "LeLe, you know it was more than a foreign excursion I was offering, right?"

Leona retrieved two cups from the cabinet. "I do, Roy."

His smile disappeared. "Can't pretend I'm not disappointed."

She slid a cup under the coffee dispenser and popped in a stout brew pod. "You're a good man, doing a good work."

"Just not good enough for you."

"I didn't say that, Roy."

"We don't have to set off on our new life until after the baby comes, if that's what's worryin' you."

"They need me."

Coffee sputtered from the spout, signifying the end of the brewing cycle.

"You know how I feel about you, LeLe. I'm not going to give up. You say you're worried about your kids, but I think you're worried you're not ready to move on." He raised his palm. "Hear me out. J.D. and Ivy would not want us to quit livin' just because they've gone on to glory."

"Roy, please."

"I won't say any more…for now. I know better than to burn bridges, especially with my support base."

If he only knew how close he'd come to the truth. "Speaking of contributors …" Leona set the steaming cup in front of Roy. "I wouldn't normally divulge church-sensitive information, but I think you deserve a heads up, a chance to round up additional support."

"Mt. Hope cutting me off?"

"You know I'd never let that happen."

"Leona, you're not the pastor's wife anymore. You can't guarantee anything."

Actually she could when it came to his financial support, but for some reason, she couldn't make herself tell him. "You and I both know that life has no guarantees, Roy."

"What's really going on here, LeLe? Did something happen while I was gone?" Roy's chest puffed up. "Did that lawyer fellow make a move on you?"

"Roy, this has nothing to do with me," Leona said, preferring not to get into her feelings for Saul. "Your support won't get cut off, but it could be drastically reduced." Leona stalled, taking time to pop the warm pod out of the machine. She didn't want to make things worse for Howard and Maxine, but Roy needed time to prepare for the possible financial changes that might be coming to his ministry. Without everyone believing it was Howard dropping the big checks in the plate, it would be harder for her to support Roy's mission without raising suspicions. "The Davises are having problems."

The Keurig sputtered in the silence.

"What kind of problems?"

"Marital. It's been a long time coming." Leona set the creamer in front of Roy. "I failed to talk Maxine off the ledge today so I have to speak to Howard tomorrow after church."

"About what?"

"About how we can help."

"Let me do it, Leona."

"They're *my* friends." Leona set her cup under the spigot. "I don't want either of them thinking I've been spreading rumors." She shoved another pod into the coffee maker and brought the lever down hard.

"My support is my business."

"Roy, this is a very fragile situation. Not only for Howard and Maxine but for the church." She jammed the brew button. "Mt. Hope Community is just barely getting back on its feet after J.D.'s death."

"That's why *you* don't need to confront Howard."

"I'm not going to *confront* him. I'm going to ask him privately how I can help him."

"Behave yourself, LeLe. Please."

"Behave myself?" She pulled her full cup out from the spigot. "I've *behaved* myself for thirty years."

"Which I'm sure J.D. appreciated."

Leona froze, both hands wrapped around the boiling

coffee. Roy had no idea what J.D. did or did not appreciate about her. But on this he was right. For years, she'd acquiesced for the sake of peace. And where had it gotten her? In this mess.

"If you're asking me to look the other way while my friends are hurting just because you don't want anything to ruin your *business*, then you've got another thing coming." Leona was hotter than the cup of coffee in her hands. "I'm *sick* of ministry as a business. I'm *sick* of behaving. And I'm *sick and tired* of you calling me LeLe."

"If I'm going to take care of you, then you're going to have to let me handle this."

Every fiber in Leona's body stiffened. "I've told you, I can take care of myself."

"How? Sellin' newspapers on the corner?"

"I'm rich, Roy. Filthy, stinkin', more-money-than-you-can-count rich!"

Roy's facial features hung limp, like she'd took a knife and slashed the wind from his sails. "What do you mean?"

"I mean J.D. made investments that have left me able to finance an entire African mission invasion if that's what I wanted."

"You sent the money?"

Hurt and shock were not looks Roy wore well. Realizing

her part in dressing him down was a deflating pinprick to her righteous anger. "Yes," she whispered.

"Why didn't you tell me?"

"Few know about the change in my financial status."

"Your lawyer friend? Does he know?"

She nodded. "Plus the kids. Mother. Roxie."

"You trust a lawyer and your neighbor, but you can't trust a man who's loved you for years." Roy shoved back from the table. "I think I better go before I say things I will regret." He stood. "I've got a sermon to prepare."

Long after the slam of the screen door had quieted, Leona sat on the kitchen stool twirling her wedding ring around and around on her finger.

Tater's nudge to her foot reminded her that the time for dwelling on the past was over. Leona climbed down, dumped her cold coffee in the sink, then went into her bedroom. Looking at the empty bed, she worked her wedding ring over her knuckle, walked to the nightstand, and opened the tackle box. She flipped the latch and lifted the lid. She stared at the empty box. "I'll always love you, J.D. But you're not here. And I don't want a cheap imitation of you." She gently laid the thin gold band where fish hooks used to be. "Goodbye, my love." She closed the lid, flipped the latch, and took the box to her closet. She put it next to the sensible brown flats she used to wear to church every Sunday.

She climbed into bed and picked up the investment book Saul had given her. She flipped to the inscription written on the title page. Her finger slowly traced the words he'd written.

You can do it, Leona.

First thing tomorrow, she'd prove Saul Levy right.

CHAPTER NINETEEN

Maxine was wringing her hands and pacing the church foyer when Leona and Maddie walked through the door. "Can I speak to you, Leona?"

"Sure."

Maxine held a flattened palm between her and Maddie and mouthed to Leona, "Alone."

Maddie gave Leona a puzzled look. "Are you ill, Maxine?"

"No," Maxine answered far too quickly. "I just need to talk to your momma for a minute."

"You're sweating." Maddie's suspicious gaze shuttled between Leona and Maxine's disheveled appearance. "Maybe I should take your pulse."

"I have my own doctor," Maxine snapped.

"Then you should see him. Soon." Maddie shot Leona a

worried look. "I'll find us some seats, Momma."

The moment Maddie started for the sanctuary, Maxine snagged Leona's arm and pulled her into the new mother's nursing room. "Did you ask Saul to represent me?"

"Have you slept since I saw you last?"

Maxine ran her hands through her stringy hair, her gaze darting between Leona and the open door. "I tried."

Leona eased the undone woman into a rocking chair. "Let me talk to Howard first, please."

"No." Maxine popped up. "If you're not going to help me get a decent lawyer, I'll have to handle this myself." She pushed past Leona.

Leona called after her but Maxine stormed through the foyer and out the front door.

Bewildered about what to do next, Leona adjusted her purse strap and headed for her pew. She walked the aisle, stopping to thank the Story sisters once again for their upstanding transportation service. Of course, she'd be happy to recommend them. In return, they assured her they'd not told a soul as to why they'd activated the prayer chain for David and Amy.

Angus and Ruthie were seated on their pew. The grins on their faces reminded Leona that she still had no idea who'd helped the boy secure his college financing. When Leona reached her new pew, the third from the front on the left, she was pleasantly surprised to see Maddie sitting next to Saul. She tapped him on the shoulder. "Good morning."

He stood and made room for her. "Good morning, Leona." Pleasure shone in his eyes. Apparently, he'd enjoyed the fries they'd shared after they left the hospital as much as she. "I saved you a seat."

Heart soaring, Leona squeezed in next to Saul. Her upper arm tingled against the smooth wool of his suit jacket. They hadn't been settled near long enough for Leona's satisfaction when Wilma Wilkerson struck a strong call to worship chord on the organ. Parker Kemp took the podium and invited everyone to stand and join him in praise. Leona couldn't resist letting her gaze slide across Saul for a glance at Maddie. According to the clock by her bedside, it had been well past midnight when Maddie came in. Maybe she and Parker had worked things out. To her disappointment, Maddie's face was a blank slate. Not one cotton-picking iota of interest twinkled in her eyes.

Leona's heart tumbled. She'd lost. Parker was going to Guatemala and Maddie was going to throw her chance of happiness away.

Her eyes still on Maddie, Leona reached for a hymnal. Her hand brushed Saul's. She pulled back with a start. "Sorry."

"I've got this." He pulled the book from the rack and turned to the page number Parker had announced. He held out the open book in a manner that suggested he was only too happy to share.

She'd not shared a hymnal since her last Sunday with J.D. Rich bass flowed easily from Saul's inviting smile. Leona cautiously clasped the corner of the book between her thumb and forefinger and joined her soprano to his.

They were well into the third verse of *On Jordan's Stormy Banks* when someone crowded in on her right. "Roy?" Leona asked between clenched teeth. "What are you doing?"

"That rental jeep is a piece of junk." Roy's wrinkled dress shirt sleeves were rolled up. Sweat plastered his dirty blonde curls to his forehead. He fumbled with the notes poking out of his Bible. He cocked his head her direction and without looking at her, whispered rather loudly, "David here?"

Leona returned her gaze to the stage. "I don't think he's coming," she whispered.

"He texted and asked if he could make an announcement before my sermon."

Leona shrugged as best she could with her shoulders pinned between two men. When the song was over, Parker asked everyone to be seated.

Roy and Saul sat first, leaving only a sliver of space

between them. Leona shot Maddie a pleading glance, hoping the girl would remember her church etiquette and scoot down to make room. Maddie's devilish grin indicated she intended to stay right where she was. To manage Leona's life for a few moments. Which Leona might have been compelled to accept had she not witnessed the great pleasure her daughter was having in seeing her mother wedged between these two men.

Howard climbed the steps to the podium and cleared his throat. Since Leona was the last one left standing and Howard obviously wasn't going to say whatever it was he had to say until she was seated, Leona had no choice but to wiggle in between Saul on her left and Roy on her right.

Cheeks aflame, Leona kept her eyes on the man in the pulpit. The elder's bald head glistened under the stage lights. With his close-set eyes and small nose, Howard's head resembled a bowling ball. Leona didn't see what Maxine saw in him. Worry that Maxine could probably start a similar rumor about Saul was quickly banished. As long as Maxine needed Saul's legal services, she'd do everything she could to remain in his good graces. For now, any budding of the relationship between her and Saul was safe.

Leona slid her hand toward her knee. She let her pinky drift toward Saul's hand resting on his knee. Their fingers touched. Neither flinched at the jolt. With military stealth, Saul intertwined his little finger with hers.

Howard removed a piece of paper from his pocket and smoothed it carefully. "As you know the Story sisters activated the prayer chain last night on behalf of David and Amy. What you may not know is …"

"What they may not know—" Maxine shouted from the back of the sanctuary. "—is what a low-down sidewinder you are, Howard Davis."

"Oh no." Leona released Saul but Roy had her so hemmed in the best she could do was glance over her shoulder. Maxine stood at the back, a big poster board clutched in her hands.

"Tell 'em, Howard," Maxine shouted. "Or I will."

Leona's gaze shot back to the pulpit.

Howard looked up from his reading. "Maxine?" Horror glazed his eyes. His chin fell to his chest. The vein at the side of his temple pulsed as if it was going to explode.

Leona whipped a glance over her shoulder. Maxine had flipped her poster over and now she was holding it high above her head.

I KNOW WHAT YOU'VE DONE … was scribbled in huge red letters.

A horrified gasp escaped Leona's lips as she tried to squirm free. "Maxine."

Roy clamped a hand on Leona's leg and held her in place. "Stay out of it, LeLe."

"I will not." Leona popped from the pew like a champagne cork.

Roy snagged her arm. "Please, LeLe," he begged under his breath.

By now everyone had turned in their pews, staring at the crying woman waving her ugly accusations like a matador flag.

"Did you think I wouldn't find out, Howard?" Maxine's voice had elevated from anger to a hawk's screech swooping in for the kill. "This is a small town. Sooner or later even the wife finds out what everyone has known all along."

"Let me go, Roy." Leona scrambled over Roy's attempt to block her exit from the row with his big feet. "Maxine. Stop!" She raced down the aisle, gathered Maxine into her arms, and used her body as a shield from the prying eyes. "Let's go home, friend." She tossed a glance over her shoulder. Howard's whitened knuckles grasped the edges of the pulpit. The color had drained from his face. Torn between whether to stick with the sobbing Maxine or race to steady the shell-shocked Howard, Leona turned toward the pulpit. "Help him."

Roy jumped to his feet.

"Not you, Roy," Leona shouted. "Saul."

CHAPTER TWENTY

Maddie had offered to sit with the heavily sedated Maxine while Leona did what she should have done when Maxine first asked, summon her courage to speak to Saul.

Leona held on to the crochet seat cover and leaned forward. "Nola Gay, take the first left into the subdivision."

Bluebird coughed and sputtered as Leona's Uber driver slowed to make the turn off the highway.

"We don't usually go outside the city limits," Etta May said, her eyes on the Google map she'd pulled up on her phone.

"Charge me extra," Leona said, offering her credit card.

"You may be rich, Leona"—Etta May gently pushed the VISA back at Leona.—"But you aren't the only one who can afford to do the Lord's work."

"What are you talking about?"

"Cotton and J.D. shared their pharmaceutical investment idea with us," Nola Gay said. "We've got a tidy little nest egg ourselves."

Maxine was right. In a small town, the wife was the last to know what everyone already knew. "Then why did you buy this used van from Howard?"

"Because we heard that the failing Mt. Hope economy had pushed Davis Cadillac into hard times."

"You bought this junk heap to help Howard out?"

"We tried to buy a new Caddy but Howard thought we couldn't afford it," Nola Gay swerved around a pothole. "A man's got to be allowed to keep his pride, Leona. He thought he was helping two old women out. We didn't have the heart to tell him otherwise."

"So this whole Uber-driver thing is your way of helping Davis Cadillac stay in business?" Was Howard using their personal funds to keep his dealership out of bankruptcy?

"We do what we can." Etta May pointed to Saul's drive. "I think that's your beau's cottage."

"Saul is not my beau."

"And some claim pharmaceuticals are not a good investment." Nola Gay eased down the drive and stopped under a big cypress. "Looks like your man's got company." She nodded toward the fender peeking out from the edge of a small shed.

"Saul is not my man."

Etta May yanked the sliding door open. "People often tell themselves whatever they must to help with their grief." She offered Leona a hand out of the van. "But sometimes the things we tell ourselves are lies. God has brought you a fine opportunity. What you do with it is up to you."

"We won't be waiting on you, Leona." Nola Gay threw the gearshift into reverse. "You'll have to find another way home."

"What happened to *Dance with the one that brung ya*?"

"You don't want to waste your life dancin' with two old windbags like us when God's handed you the perfect fella for spinnin' you around." Nola Gay floored it and the tire slung gravel at Leona's feet.

Leona could hear the twins cackling over the roar of the Bluebird until the black smoke disappeared from sight.

A lizard sunned himself on the stone path that Leona followed to the porch. She knocked on the screen. "Saul?" She waited, listening to water gently lapping the shore. "Saul?" She knocked again, this time casting her gaze toward the dock.

"Ugh." Saul's boat was not moored to any of the pilings. "Not the water."

Leona took a deep breath and navigated the terrace

stones. At the lake's edge, she raised her hand to shield her eyes from the sun. Heart thundering in her ears, she scanned the peaceful view. In the distance, she spotted a boat. Two occupants.

She tried waving to get their attention but the shade from the trees made it impossible for her to be seen. She pulled her phone from her purse. No bars. She could wait until darkness forced Saul back to shore. But it was at least an hour until sunset. She didn't want to risk Maxine waking up and causing Maddie who-knows-what kind of trouble. If she wanted to talk to Saul, she had no choice but to walk the length of the dock and hope that from the platform she could possibly be seen.

She set a tentative sandaled foot on the first board. "Lord, help me." Keeping her eyes on the shorter man in the boat, she took one step after another and tried not to think about how deep the water was below here. Before she knew it, she was at the deck's edge. "Saul!" Her voice carried over the water. "Saul!" She waved her arms. The shorter man in the boat waved a towel as a signal she'd been heard.

Standing on the platform, she watched the boat speed to her. Within minutes, Saul was cutting the motor and letting the boat drift on the waves easing it toward its mooring place.

"Howard?" Leona's surprise at Saul's fishing partner reached the men before their boat had completely reached the dock.

Howard jerked the bill of his cap over the embarrassment flushing his face. "Leona."

She'd asked Saul to look after Howard, but she'd meant help him stagger down from the podium, not bring him out to the lake for an afternoon of male bonding. Howard's prolonged presence could only mean one thing. "Have you hired Saul to represent you in the divorce?"

"Divorce?" Howard's head snapped up. "What divorce?"

It was all Leona could do to keep from clawing that surprised innocence from Howard's face. "The one Maxine's sure you're going to want after what she pulled today."

"I want to wring her neck, not divorce her."

"He's here at my invitation." Saul tossed Leona a rope. "After what Howard's been through, I thought he could use an afternoon of rest and relaxation."

"What Howard's been through?" Leona snugged the boat against a piling. "What about poor Maxine? She believes you're having an affair, Howard."

"An affair?" Howard's shoulders deflated. He didn't move. Just sat in the boat sadly shaking his head. "When would I have the time or the energy to have an affair?"

"Then what *have* you been doing with the money?"

Even that didn't perk Howard up and money always piqued

Howard's interest. Instead, he rubbed the bristles of the five o'clock shadow on his face. "Keeping Davis Cadillac out of bankruptcy court."

What the Story sisters had said was true. The Davis fortune was in danger. Leona's punctured ire dissipated in a long, pained sigh. "Why didn't you tell her?"

Howard slowly lifted his head. "You, of all people, should know that you don't *tell* Maxine anything she doesn't want to hear."

Saul climbed out of the boat. "Come on, Howard." With a heave, Saul hauled the broken man to the dock. "Drop by the office tomorrow. We'll work something out with your creditors."

Leona waited on the dock while Saul helped Howard trudge up the bank and get into his car.

Saul's face looked none too happy as he navigated the terrace steps and walked the dock where she stood holding the rope to a boatload of questions.

"If you're going to represent Howard, I guess that negates my reason for coming," she said.

"Why don't you let me be the judge of that?" Saul took the rope from her hand and wrapped it around a metal cleat. "Lemonade?"

She held up a warning finger. "Last time I drank your homemade concoction I ended up dancing on the water."

Eyes alight with admiration, Saul looked at her feet. "You're standing pretty solidly on your own."

Was she? She and the Davises had been at odds since Colton died. While she and J.D. had taken the brunt of Howard and Maxine's grief, Leona had never wished another loss upon them. Yet, as she watched Howard's taillights disappear into the twilight, sadness overtook her. The Davis marriage was falling apart. She owed it to Maxine to do her best to help her pick up the pieces.

Leona surveyed the water surrounding her on three sides. Wind rippled the surface, but the waves in her stomach were beginning to calm. Instead of feeling trapped, a sense of protection enveloped her. She straightened her shoulders and gave a weary smile. "Only by God's grace."

"It's the only way any of us stand." Saul held out his hand. "Come on."

She stared at his offered hand. "I think you should know that I came here on Maxine's behalf. To ask you to agree to become her divorce attorney."

"I don't do divorces."

"And I don't usually help someone seek the dissolution of their marriage. But I'm at a loss on how to proceed."

"Have time to sit on the porch?"

"My Uber drivers dumped me and ran. So if you're not

willing to give me a lift back to town, I've got to start walking."

"Wouldn't get far in those shoes."

She glanced down at the hemp wedges she'd chosen to compliment her creamy linen capris. "Then you better keep it short," she said, knowing full-well she'd sit on his porch all night if he was going to open up.

A few minutes later they were settled in two comfy bentwood chairs, a pitcher of lemonade champagne between them. Leona picked at the cheese on the cutting board, determined to wait Saul out for an explanation.

After what seemed forever, Saul rose and sent an apple core skipping across the water. His eyes fixed on where the core had sunk, he began to speak, "Before Claire got diagnosed with breast cancer, we were both very intent on making the most of our careers. No children. No strings to tie us down. But as I advanced, I became less and less likely to take the time out to reconnect. My calls to her were fewer and shorter. I took less leave than I had coming." He sat, heavy and weary. He leaned forward and rested his elbows on his knees. He rubbed his palms as if smoothing out what he had to say next. "So while I was making rank, Claire found someone who would give her the attention she deserved. Three months later, she filed for divorce." He fell back in his chair. "I was hurt, but thought maybe she was right. That we were better suited apart. And then she got sick. I said, 'Let your lover take care of you.' She said, 'He left.'" Saul stroked the shadowed stubble on his face. "She said, 'I want to go home.'"

"What did you say?"

"The only thing I could. 'I'm on my way.'" He took a heavy breath. "In less than a week, we'd both left the military. Sold everything we owned. I bought an RV and brought her here. To recover on her land. Living together, for the first time in our ten years of marriage, wasn't easy. We were both so angry at the other's unwillingness to sacrifice earlier."

Leona was torn between wanting to say something comforting and holding him, but a small voice in her head was telling her to keep quiet. To listen.

"I was going to start working on the house, but I spent the next two years, driving Claire to Dallas three times a week because of Mt. Hope's lack of proper medical care. The trips nearly killed her."

Saul's watery eyes found Leona's. "Taking care of my wife, making up for all the years I'd chosen my career over her, was the best thing I've ever done." He drifted back into his memories. "Supporting her. Loving her. All of it changed my life. It was an honor greater than serving my country." He took a pained breath. "Toward the end, she suffered greatly. When she died, I thought I would be relieved. That I'd sell this house she'd never lived in and I'd never look back. Instead, I was so broken I wanted to jump off the end of the dock."

"I know the feeling," Leona whispered.

"I know you do, but you don't know this." Saul turned his gaze to the water. "One evening, I was standing with my toes on the very edge of that platform when a larger-than-life man named J.D. Harper motored into my cove."

"J.D.?" Leona whispered.

Saul nodded. "He must have sensed something was wrong because he asked if he could come ashore and cool off in my shade. The more my gaze drifted toward the water, the more determined he became to stay. Said his wife didn't like the water, but she was used to his fishing until all hours of the night." Saul's demeanor lightened. "J.D. noticed the house, overgrown and neglected. He said, 'We can fix that. Restore it to something even better than it was before.' I told him I didn't have a reason to live here anymore. He said, 'Well, you can't sell like this.' On his days off, he'd show up with his tool box and a fishing pole."

Leona's mind ricocheted from Saul's story to memories of helping J.D. pack his fishing cooler with extra sandwiches and soft drinks. She'd pat his expanding middle and tease him about taking so much food. He just laughed and claimed a man could develop a powerful hunger on the water. It'd never occurred to her that her husband had been rebuilding a house and a broken man. Unable to speak, Leona waited on Saul to finish the story, a story she had to hear.

As if Saul sensed her desperation, he continued, "J.D. loved to laugh, but he never pried. Little by little I began to trust him, to believe he was my friend. Then one day, he told me about another carpenter…one who lived two thousand years ago…the master carpenter whose specialty was restoration."

The image of J.D. sitting on this very porch, his worn Bible in his calloused hands, a twinkle in his eyes as he walked Saul through the ancient stories that had meant everything to him, cracked the dam holding back Leona's tears.

"Howard and Maxine can recover from this, Leona." Saul offered Leona a napkin then refilled their glasses. "I'll help them salvage their credit, but I won't help them divorce."

Leona blew her nose, fully aware that mascara probably ringed her eyes. "Thank you."

"Thank you?"

"For reminding me."

"That J.D. was a remarkable man?"

"Yes."

"There's not a person in Mt. Hope who would say

otherwise."

"Except for Howard and Maxine."

Saul snorted surprised agreement. "Except for them."

Sun-kissed rays outlined dark lavender clouds hovering above the western shore. Leona and Saul sat in silence, soaking in the glorious reminder of God's presence. When the last of the light faded, the cicadas stirred and the dock lights sputtered to life.

Saul lit the citronella candle on the rugged coffee table. "I can't offer you a life of saving the world." His reference to Roy and his African adventure proposal was not lost on her. "But I can do this." He lifted the corner of the cheese tray and pulled out a business-sized envelope. "Open it."

"And just when I was beginning to believe you weren't the man of mystery everyone says you are."

Leona lifted the flap, extracted a folded piece of paper, and held it close to the candle's flame. The letterhead bore a medical symbol and the name Robin Boyer, M.D., Maternal-Fetal Medicine, Dallas, Texas.

"What in the world?" Leona's eyes devoured the brief contents. By the time she finished the last line she wasn't breathing. "You convinced Mt. Hope's medical board to hire a specialist for Amy?"

"Not just for Amy. The plan is to add a bevy of specialists, doctors adept at treating anyone who faces difficult medical circumstances."

"How did you get her to agree to come?"

"I incorporated your suggestions in the proposal." He tapped the letter. "You're missing the most important part. She said yes."

"Who's paying for this?"

"Me."

"You?"

"In keeping with my resolution to be so transparent that you'll have no choice but to trust me, I'll confess that J.D. was more than my friend. He was my business partner. I had more cash to invest in his little pharmaceutical adventure, which means my wealth is considerably greater than yours."

Leona couldn't contain her surprised laughter.

"What's so funny?" Saul asked.

She couldn't tell him David thought he was only interested in her for her money. Especially, since she'd done everything she could to douse his interest. "I can't let you pay for all of this."

"Are you afraid the folks of Mt. Hope will discover I have a heart?"

She laughed. "I'm afraid you'll get the big head and take all the credit for saving the babies and mothers of this county."

His lips curved into a smile. "You can build the hospital wing." He was enjoying seeing her drop her guard. "Fair enough?"

"Deal." She stuck out her hand and he shook it firmly. Before she let him go, she asked, "Is Angus Crouch going to school on a scholarship or did *you* finance his education?"

Saul burst out laughing, raising his free hand in surrender. "You can buy the kid a car." He lowered his hand slowly. "Does that make you happy?"

Leona folded the letter and slid it back into the envelope. "You didn't have to do this."

"When I saw the terror on your face that day I brought David to the emergency room, the only thing I could think to do for you was step outside and make a few calls. The decision was made and approved by the hospital board before I offered to buy you dinner."

That he'd picked up the phone and made the very thing she wanted happen quickened her breath. "Since we're both in such a spending mood, why don't we build Kendra a new dance studio?"

One brow quirked in amused interest. "Something with a deck over the water?"

Leona leaned closer. "Don't get carried away."

"A fountain in the atrium then?"

"She does have all those kids to consider. It would be awful if one fell in."

"Maybe we should do an enclosed aquarium?"

Leona felt her smile growing with each adjustment to their growing plan. "Better."

"All anonymously, of course."

"Of course," she agreed, her gaze buried in his.

The breaking of a twig drew their attention to the water's edge. A doe and her fawn stepped into the glow of the dock's lights. The doe's ears twitched on high alert.

"I've been spreading corn for a year now," Saul whispered. "She comes every night, but it has taken a long time for her to finally trust me."

They sat in silence, each afraid to breathe for fear of sending the deer bounding into the brush. When at last the doe and her fawn had drunk their fill, they turned and quietly disappeared into the thick undergrowth.

Saul stood and offered Leona his hand. "One last dance before you're off to see the world."

"Off to see the world?"

"With Roy." Saul's smile was tight, and pain-filled, but ripe with nothing but best wishes for her. "Now that Amy has the medical care she needs, I can supervise our construction projects. That'll leave you free to go and save the world."

He was right. In one fell swoop, he'd taken care of her all of her reasons, and her excuses, for staying in Mt. Hope.

All except one.

Leona stood. "There's much to do around the world, that's true." She closed the gap between them, her lips only inches from his. "But I know I'll never achieve anything worthwhile if I leave my heart here." She wrapped both arms around his neck and kissed him.

The gentle brush of his mustache against her lips awakened a new and unknown world, a place filled with her heart's desires. And who would have thought she would find what she'd been looking for in her own backyard?

With cicadas buzzing in her ears, everything, but the taste of a satisfied life, fell away. Joy swelled in her heart.

When at last their lips parted, Leona smiled. She held up her right hand. "Dance with me, Saul Levy."

CHAPTER TWENTY-ONE

A jazz band played on the lighted terrace overlooking the lake. A pleasant autumn breeze fluttered the checkered cloths that draped long tables heaped with barbecued brisket and corn on the cob. From the size of the crowd milling about the property, the entire town of Mt. Hope had turned out to celebrate the wedding of Leona Harper and the county's toughest lawyer. Maddie stood on the porch watching a man she barely knew twirl her glowing mother around the dock.

Aunt Roxie handed Maddie a glass of spiked lemonade. "Can you believe your momma is dancing on water?"

Maddie choked on the tart irony. "I've seen the woman walk on water."

Roxie raised her glass in agreement. "I'm glad she finally believes she can get herself back to shore."

Balancing on one foot, Maddie slipped out of her heels and held the straps in the crook of her finger. "Does that mean I'm off the hook if the family car ever careens over a bridge?"

"It's the freedom you've always wanted, right?"

Maddie set her glass on a nearby table. "Right."

"Then why so glum? I thought you and David had given your mother your blessing."

"We did."

"And?"

"We're glad Momma's happy." Maddie's gaze drifted toward David and Parker at the horseshoe pit. "I just want her to *stay* happy."

Roxie's head turned toward Maddie's target. "So she'll leave you alone?"

"Don't think I don't know what Momma did." Maddie watched Parker and David haggle over whose turn it was.

"You mean scheduling her wedding before Parker set off for South America so you could see him one last time?"

"That's exactly what I mean."

"We had to hoof it, that's for sure."

Maddie glared at Roxie. "You're evil."

"Hell's bells, darlin'. Everybody knows that. If you don't believe it, just ask Maxine." She nodded to where Maxine and Howard stood apart from the crowd, their arms crossed and scowls on their faces. "It's still touch and go with those two."

Maddie pulled at her maid of honor wrist corsage. "Who wears these things anymore?" She scattered the petals over Saul's well-manicured lawn.

"He loves me. He loves me not." Aunt Roxie chanted as the petals floated to the ground.

"I don't know what to do, Aunt Roxie."

"Baby, if you don't want Parker, give him your blessing and let him go." Roxie gently turned Maddie and pointed her in the direction of the horseshoe game. "Get it done, and I promise it'll get your momma off your back."

"If only it was a question of not wanting him." Maddie handed Roxie her shoes, picked up the small purse Momma claimed went perfectly with her bridal party dress, and stepped off the porch.

The cool grass pressing between her toes was a stark contrast to the fire burning hot inside of her. She'd tried to forget Parker. But he was a complicated equation of goofy smiles, an obsession with botany, and these crazy, irrational dreams of saving the ecosystem of a third-world country, an equation she'd yet to solve. Parker loved small towns. She wanted a life in the city. Parker was laid-back and low-keyed. She was high-strung and adrenaline-driven. Parker wanted a family. She never wanted to be tied down.

She'd moved the variables around and around, but the truth was, there were far too many facts for the combination of Maddie Harper plus Parker Kemp to ever work out. Aunt Roxie was right. Parker deserved to be happy. If she truly loved him, she had to let him go.

Maddie padded barefoot down to the sandpit, the skirt of her maid of honor dress swirling just above her knees. She picked up a stray horseshoe. "Is this a testosterone-only game?"

"You can have my turn, little sister." David stepped away from the stake. "I need to check on Amy."

"I saw her at the meat table."

"Again?" David shook his head. "I'm beginning to worry that our baby is going to be a beef cake."

Maddie and Parker exchanged amused glances. Not because what David had said was funny, but because they couldn't believe how much Amy and this baby meant to the man who couldn't decide what he wanted in life.

"She's doing great, David," Maddie reassured. "I checked her numbers myself before the wedding."

"You'll come back when the little guy is born, right?" David asked.

Maddie nodded. "I'll be on the first plane."

Parker elbowed Maddie. "Way to make me feel guilty."

"No guilt, man." David clapped Parker on the back. "Someone's got to save the world." David handed Maddie his horseshoe. "I'm leaving that up to you two."

Maddie and Parker stood side by side as David jogged up the terrace steps in search of his very pregnant wife.

"I wish …" Parker paused.

Maddie's chest squeezed. She turned to him. "Wish what?"

He looked at her, not just at her face, but deep into her soul. "Nothing."

Maddie started to reach for the coal black curl falling over the tiny scar on his forehead; the one he'd acquired the night he rescued her in a blizzard and his truck spun out. He pulled back slightly and Maddie lowered her hand.

"Momma says you're leaving tomorrow."

Parker shifted his horseshoe from hand to hand. "Got the renters settled on my ranch, so I guess I'm ready."

"Nervous?"

"Excited."

Parker had dreamed of helping people become proficient in feeding themselves for years.

"Daddy always said a person should follow their calling."

"I learned a lot about faith from Reverend Harper." From the glimmer of peace in Parker's dark eyes, he was doing exactly what he'd been born to do. For her to try to mold him to fit her needs would be like someone asking her to walk away from medicine. She couldn't do it. Not for anything or anyone.

"I got you a little something." Maddie fiddled with the clasp on her bag, but her hands were shaking so badly she couldn't get it open. She thrust her purse at Parker. "It's inside."

He dropped his horseshoe on the toe of his boot. As he hopped around, laughing to keep from trying not to howl in pain, Maddie couldn't help but laugh. Two things in life she could always count on. Parker Kemp would always be clumsy and he would always make her laugh.

"Are you okay?"

When he finally shook off the pain, he looked at the purse she still was asking him to open. "Is something going to jump out at me?"

"That snake trick was so junior high."

"You haven't changed that much." He undid the clasp and hurriedly thrust the purse back at her.

"Chicken." Maddie opened her bag and pulled out a pocket-sized paperback. When she placed it in his hands, she couldn't help but remember how those same hands had willingly helped her and others so many times.

He turned the book over and studied the cover. "A plant

guide?"

"In Spanish."

"It's perfect." His Adam's apple bobbed up and down as he tucked it into his shirt pocket and she knew he was swallowing waves of emotion. Same as her. He patted the bulge on his chest as if he was trying to keep his heart from falling out. "Guess this is goodbye then?"

"Guess so." She bit the corner of her lip and nodded slightly. "Parker ..."

"Yeah?" Hopeful expectation sounded in his whisper.

"Don't make me come down there and save your butt."

****

Noooooo! Please tell me it isn't so! This can't be goodbye for Maddie and Parker, can it?

It seems reasonable to believe Leona will be so busy enjoying her new life with Saul Levy that she won't have the time or inclination to continue interfering in David and Maddie's lives. But then, we all know Leona, don't we?

Besides the fate of Maddie and Parker, there are so many other questions left unanswered. Does David and Amy's baby boy arrive safely? Can Howard and Maxine save their failing marriage? What happens to Ruthie after Angus goes off to college? Can the Story sisters Uber forever? And then there's the new doctor in town. What if Dr. Robin Boyer was not the woman everyone was expecting?

If you can't leave Mt. Hope without knowing the rest of the story, you'll be happy to know, you can join thousands of readers who are taking advantage of the happy ending that is just one click away. Grab your copy of **BABY SHOES** today.

Sign up for your **FREE** sneak peek at **BABY SHOES**, the next installment of the Mt. Hope Adventure series at Lynne Gentry's **JOIN THE ADVENTURE** newsletter **@www.lynngentry.com**. This occasional update allows you exclusive information on releases, contests, and insider tidbits.

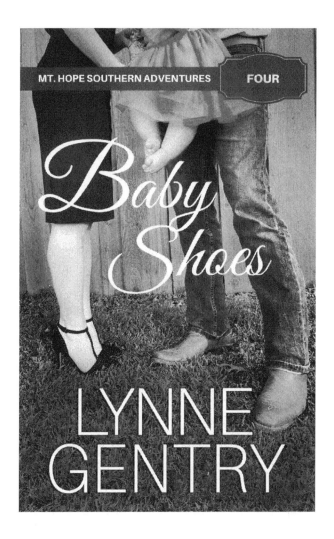

Aren't the people of Mt. Hope fun? If you enjoyed escaping into the community of Mt. Hope, you'll be happy to know your adventure doesn't have to end with **DANCING SHOES**.

The fourth book in the Mt. Hope Southern Adventures series, **BABY SHOES** is in the works and will be available soon.

Have you read the first book in the series? If not, here's your opportunity to catch up. You'll love **WALKING SHOES.**

Enjoy this book? YOU can make a BIG difference.

Reviews are the most powerful tools in my arsenal when it comes to getting attention for my books. When loyal readers share their enthusiasm and their reviews, it is secret gold to a book's ranking. I'm very grateful every time a reader tells their friends about this series and leaves a review. I'm grateful for you, dear reader.

About the Author

Lynne Gentry knew marrying a preacher might change her plans. She didn't know how ministry would change her life. An author of numerous novels, short stories, and dramatic works, Lynne travels the country as a professional acting coach and inspirational speaker. Because Lynne's imagination loves to run wild, she also writes in the fantasy/science fiction genre of time travel. You can come along on the adventures she takes into historical worlds at **www.lynnegentry.com** Lynne loves spending time with her family and her medical therapy dog.

Let's connect on FaceBook @AuthorLynneGentry or via my website, www.lynnegentry.com, so you'll always be the first to know about new releases.

Thanks for joining the Harper family on this leg of their Mt. Hope Adventure. I hope you'll take the next leg with Leona in BABY SHOES, available soon wherever good books are sold.